Driving the Heart

Driving the Heart
and other stories

Jason Brown

W. W. Norton & Company
New York London

Printed in the United States of America
First Edition

The text of this book is composed in Bembo
with the display set in Mrs. Eaves
Manufacturing by Courier Companies, Inc.
Book design and desktop composition by Lane Kimball Trubey

Library of Congress Cataloging-in-Publication Data

Brown, Jason, 1969–
Driving the heart, and other stories / Jason Brown.
p. cm.
ISBN 978-0-393-33206-3
I. United States—Social life and customs—20th century—Fiction.
I. Title
PS3552.R685674D75 1999
813'.54—dc21 98-37725
CIP

W. W. Norton & Company, Inc., 500 Fifth Avenue, New York, N.Y. 10110
http://www.wwnorton.com

W. W. Norton & Company Ltd., 10 Coptic Street, London WC1A 1PU

1 2 3 4 5 6 7 8 9 0

Acknowledgments

The author wishes to thank the following people and institutions for making this book possible: Frank Burroughs, George Smith, Dan Riedman, Cornell University, Maureen McCoy, Robert Morgan, A. R. Ammons, Alison Lurie, Dan McCall, Dylan Willoughby, the Saltonstahl Foundation, Stanford University, the Capote Foundation, John L'Heureux, Tabitha Griffin, Andrew Blauner, Susan Ketchin, Susan Hahn, and Lois Rosenthal.

These stories have appeared in the following publications:

Animal Stories
Georgia Review
25 and Under/Fiction
(Norton/DoubleTakeBooks)

•

The Coroner's Report
TriQuarterly

•

Detox
Columbia

•

The Dog Lover
25 and Under/Fiction
(Norton/DoubleTakeBooks)

•

Driving the Heart
Best American Short Stories 1996
Mississippi Review

•

Halloween
Columbia

•

Hydrophobia
Indiana Review

•

The Naked Running Boy
Epoch

•

Sadness of the Body
TriQuarterly

•

Thief
Story

Contents

Driving the Heart

Driving the Heart

Traveling between Danvers and Natick yesterday I saw a man in a flower truck drive by at 80 m.p.h. with his eyes closed. I turned to Dale, a guy the hospital hired for me to train, and said, "Nothing, not even someone's liver, is that important." He put his hand on top of the metal case marked *Liver* and nodded.

We drive the no-rush jobs, eyeballs, livers, morphine, or kidneys, through the day traffic to or from the airport. Sometimes when a patient decides to die at home and runs out of painkillers, we will bring extra morphine out to them at night. Tonight we are driving way out to Lebanon Springs, to the town where I was born, with a heart for a woman about to die from some accident or some disease. Hearts travel at night.

Dale sits next to me holding the metal box marked *Heart*. His eyes droop. His head leans to the right. Next thing he'll be sleeping, dreaming down the highway. I know what it's like.

When the weather is foul like tonight and the airplane can't make it, they send us. We're the only choice they have of reaching such a small town in such an out-of-the-way place. Cellular phone service is out and in many places the power is out, but most of the regular pay phones still work. We stop every hour at designated places and call the hospital to make sure the patient in Lebanon is still alive. The hospital is in contact with Lebanon. We are not allowed to stop for food or drink and, if we can help it, even to urinate on this six-hour journey. We make the call and if she's still alive we rush on. If not then we can pause briefly for food and bathroom before we turn around and drive without stopping for Worcester, where a plane will take the heart to some other person in a city with a major airport. This heart, however, is getting old. There probably won't be time to take it anywhere after Lebanon.

Hearts are packed in ice. But even a frozen heart will only last for twenty-four hours on the outside, unofficially. That's why if we have to take it to Worcester, there will only be time to fly the heart to a major airport, then rush it from there by helicopter to a hospital in the same city. There is always a patient. Driving to Lebanon, we shoot for six or seven hours at the most. Tonight we have to hurry through the high winds and beating rain, in order not to waste this heart.

I stop the car and have Dale run out through the rain to the pay phone with the number I gave him.

"What's her name?" he asks.

"You won't be talking to her," I say, "and it doesn't matter. Just give the hospital the job number. They'll say drive on if she's still alive, or turn around."

A few minutes later he comes running back, gets in the car, brushes the rain off his sleeves, and nods his head. After a few more minutes he says, "I'm hungry," even though I've already explained the rules.

Hospital delivery often attracts people like myself, who have cared very deeply about the wrong things. Who, in less than half an average life span, have been born, born again, arrested for armed robbery, and born once more. A person can only be born so many times before even the Christians don't want to take you seriously. The second time I was born I was twenty years old and lying in a donated suit on the floor of a jail in Sturgis, Michigan. I remember one of the officers brought me a bowl of stew and suggested I eat something before going into court, but I shook my head. I was being charged with driving under the influence and assaulting a police officer, although I didn't remember doing those things. The judge informed me that I had drunk ten ounces of 151 in a few hours. He lowered his head after this announcement, not because I was a startling case, but because I was the same kind of case he saw day after day and he was tired. I asked what I could do to show him that I had finally gotten the picture, that all I wanted was one more chance. He looked at me and laughed, which was to say: that's what everybody says. He didn't know that I was reborn, that over in Grass Lake, where I wanted to go after I was released, people believed.

We drive all over New England, sometimes to New York, but mostly we stay around the Boston area. If you know the Wenham-Woburn-Needham-Braintree route, then you know that the places to live are Belmont, Weston, Concord, or beyond but not so far out as Lowell. All the names up and down the coast, Weekapaug, Quonochontaug, Naquit, Teaticket, Menauhaunt, and Falmouth Heights, remind me of the life I could have had if things had been different. I have a friend living that life over in Sakonnet right now. I go over and visit him once in a while—from his second-floor bathroom window a sliver of ocean can be seen.

Dale reaches over and turns the radio up; he leans on his right elbow against the window. He slumps in his seat. I turn the radio back down. No amount of training will make a kid like this understand his job. Even as the passenger you should sit alert. Someone else's life sits in your hands. His head nods against the passenger window as I flick the radio off. "No more radio," I say. That wakes him up. Dale straightens himself and asks what happened to the woman who needs the heart, but I can tell by the way he fiddles with the buttons on his coat that he doesn't really care. I tell him I don't know, that the woman could be thirty, could be seventy. Could be heart disease, could be anything, they never tell me. Usually they take the heart from someone who is alive but brain-dead and transport it to someone whose thoughts are clear but whose heart is dead. And in truth, I explain, they usually give preference to the young. The moment the heart leaves the body of the donor, it is cross-clamped and the clock starts ticking. In the Lebanon hospital they are standing there in the operating room right now, smocked and ready, waiting for us. Dale nods and we drive on in silence.

I roll the window down for a moment to let in some air and then roll it back up again. I turn to Dale: "A man in Abilene, Texas, gets drunk and drives his car through a 7-Eleven. Three hours later his heart travels on a plane bound for Logan Airport. Six hours later his heart sits next to you in a large silver case marked *Heart*, and we are driving down the highway at the speed limit toward some supine client in a hospital room asleep or possibly in a coma who will not live another day without this heart. This," I say to Dale, "is the importance of your job." He nods, furrowing his brow. No matter how many times I explain, I don't think he will understand.

"What if something goes wrong?" he asks.

"Nothing will go wrong if you don't get any ideas. Now go make the call," I say, pointing at the variety store.

I live in a so-so neighborhood. The people there smell and never take out the trash. I look out my window at a funeral home. For four months each year the sun rarely shines in this part of the country. Some mornings I consider the consequences of quitting my job and doing nothing for the rest of my life. People will still get their organs and their drugs, driven here and there by someone like myself. A replacement. The hospital has them. The only thing that will happen differently in the world if I quit my job is that I will not be able to eat.

I ask Dale if he has ever donated an organ. He shakes his head, looks at me in silence, and then we sit there, ahead of schedule, thinking. I feel like telling him to keep his eyes open.

I've seen some strange things. A woman from Nova Scotia once came into the hospital and offered to sell two kidneys. She said she had four. The doctor on duty said he was interested in such a claim, but that it was the hospital's policy, the law in fact, not to accept such offers.

I know what it's like to want things. I've always wanted to travel the world but probably never will. I've seen pictures. I've always wanted to date a very beautiful woman.

Only once have I flown in an airplane, crossing the water to London with a case of hospital files to be signed by a man there. Somewhere out over Labrador the pregnant woman across the aisle started to scream. The husband started running up and down the aisle while his wife was pulling on her seat and pushing with her knees against the people in front, her stomach seizing with contractions. The man suddenly whipped around, focused on me, and yelled, "I need a doctor! Is anyone a doctor?" A woman sitting in back came forward saying she used to be a nurse. The man stepped aside, pointing at his wife in her light cotton floral dress, the makeup washing down onto her neck. "She's only seven months—not even," the husband said. When he stepped aside a little more to allow the nurse to move in, I could see liquid from between the pregnant woman's legs pouring off her seat and onto the floor. The woman who used to be a nurse looked directly away, holding her head with her hand. She was looking at me and through me. "How much time before we land?" the man blurted at the stewardess, who had just arrived. "Too much time," the ex-nurse, looking at me, said.

The most exciting thing that can be said about me is that I delivered pizzas in dangerous neighborhoods when I lived in New York. How I can be both obsessed and relaxed at the same time is a mystery to me, but I consider it one of my greatest accomplishments. I'm not very old, but I would say that so far nothing has gone according to plan, that people have been unpredictable and that's about the extent of it. I would also say that certain ideas seem basically true to me. You cannot serve two masters well. Our thoughts are of little consequence. Live cautiously. You have to in my family. Back when I was twelve, for instance, I was traveling down Capisic Street in Lebanon when a woman traveling thirty, forty miles an hour hit the rear tire of my bike. I rolled over the hood and the roof, bounced off the trunk, and landed standing on my feet. She screeched to a stop and broke out weeping on the steering wheel, afraid to look. I walked up and tapped on her window. Her fingers danced on the dashboard. She looked at me. "Are you all right?" I asked. "I don't believe it," the woman said, resting her head back down on the wheel. "I don't believe it."

The road we're traveling down tonight feels familiar, the rhythm of the bumps and ruts against the tires, but in the dark nothing looks the same. Dale fumbles with the map, turning it toward the window so he can read with the help of an occasional streetlight. "Where is this place we're going to?" he asks.

"Lebanon Springs."

"It's not on the map," Dale says.

"What?" I ask.

"Lebanon."

"Turn it over. It's on the other side." Dale turns the map over and brings it up close to his face. "Find the green line I made. It starts in Boston; follow to where it ends."

"I found it," he says. "It's tiny. There can't be much to this town."

"There's a woman who needs a heart," I say. "That's all you need to know."

Some people say I was thinking too much and some people say I wasn't thinking enough, but I probably just wasn't thinking about the right things. Don't take advice from yourself, don't leave your apartment without a good reason, don't have a telephone, don't own too many things, don't own too few. Live on the first floor. Watch out for people.

Dale lets out a long sigh. He runs his hands through his slicked-back hair, then rubs the back of his neck. Dale is wrong for the job. There's no use even getting to know him because I'll just be training someone new next week and asking all the same questions, explaining all the same rules.

Dale asks if he can look at the heart, to see how it's kept alive. He thinks it might be helpful for the job, but I think otherwise. Does he think I haven't sat alone in this seat next to a case marked *Heart* and not looked inside? There's nothing to look at. It either works or it doesn't.

I turn to Dale: "You've read the manual?"

He nods, but I'm not sure he even knows what manual I'm talking about.

"You get to one of the designated stops only to find that the phone is out. What do you do? Stop at the next phone along the road or drive on? No time to think. Page fifty-two of the manual, right?"

"Stop at the next phone," he says. "The next phone along the road, I mean."

"I know what you mean and you're wrong. You drive on." I let him fiddle with the glove compartment handle and crack his knuckles. "When in doubt," I tell him, "always drive on. Just remember that one thing, all right? All right?"

"All right," he says.

He looks out the window. I look briefly where he's looking, but the shape of the hills on the horizon depends on the phase of the moon. I don't recognize a thing. On a night like tonight when the moon is hidden by the storm, we can only recognize the windshield wipers, the sheets of rain, and the vague shape of the white road sign letters. We could be headed anywhere. The last time I traveled down this road I was hitchhiking home and ended up in a car accident. I told a guy and a girl who picked me up on Route 302 somewhere that I would go as far as they were going. He told me that they were headed for her parents' house in a little town out where 302 turns into 89, called Lebanon Springs. I nodded, and he drove faster than the speed limit. I had been outside in the snow for too long, and my feet were numb. I took off my shoes in the backseat and rubbed each toe, worried that they might not come back. Suddenly there was a thud, breaking glass, and we slid into the guardrail. The head of a large buck had smashed against the windshield, spraying glass shards onto the driver, whose head rested against the steering wheel. I crawled out the back door. The tiny glass fragments melted into the bottoms of my bare feet. The guy's girlfriend had to crawl out her window and over the hood. She walked toward me, swaying her hips like a model, rubbing her head. The deer stood in front of the car watching us. Then he closed his eyes. I never made it back to Lebanon that time.

In the dawn haze I start to recognize sections of forest from the last time I was here, eight years ago. We'll enter from the east side of town, so we won't have to use the Thurman Bridge, where I was born crossing over from Stockton in a Pinto, my father behind the wheel and my mother sprawled out in back. The story goes that my mother said she wasn't going to make it, and my father said she had to wait. She said she couldn't and there was much screaming. She wanted something to kill the pain. He told her just to think about something else and hold it in and then before she knew it they would be there. But all she knew was that she couldn't wait another second, and I was born at 11:42 p.m., before we even crossed the river.

Staring through the rain-splattered windshield into the dark gray forest, I am reminded of the same forest twenty miles from here, where I lived with my parents at the end of a long dirt road. We lived there for five or six years, but one morning it was so cold that the storm pane cracked down the middle and fell into the backyard. I woke up and wandered into my parents' bathroom, waiting for them to wake, stepped up on a stool, opened the medicine cabinet, and pulled down a box of razor blades hidden from me behind the shaving cream. Taking out two, I placed one in the palm of my right hand, then squeezed my fingers shut. With my left hand I ran the other blade lightly, painlessly up and down my arm from the shoulder to the palm. It was so long ago, I don't remember what I was thinking. The little slits remained dry for a second, caught off guard, before red lines appeared and eventually washed together like flooding rivers. I walked into their bedroom, groping my hand along the wall for the light switch. Her head bolted up. Then I found the light switch.

Several years later—I can't remember how many; we must have lived there for more than seven years—I was ten years old standing at the same window, my father having been gone from the house for quite some time, I heard my mother's faltering footsteps climbing the stairs. I locked my bedroom door, pushed one of the chairs up against the knob, and then returned to the window. I heard the floorboards creak as she crept up to the door and carefully, trying not to wake me, turned the doorknob and pushed forward. When the door would not open, she pushed more frantically and cursed under her breath. The rain splashed against the window.

It has stopped raining now and the sky has started to lighten. Dale runs off into Ken's Variety, twenty miles east of our destination, to make our last call. Twenty minutes to go. I decide that when Dale returns I'll ask him some questions about his life, about the letter D sewn onto his high school jacket, about what he wants to do with his life after this. I should try to be nice.

Maybe he wants to live over in Wayland or Lexington and summer down at Marion or Pocasset, slightly off the beaten path, where it's warm and the grass comes right down to the ocean and the beaches keep going. It sounds like a good life to me.

I hear a car engine gearing down behind me and then the grumble of the braking wheels against the gravel of the shoulder. Two guys pull up beside my window in a pickup. The truck weaves a little as it comes to a stop. The driver rolls down his window, spits out some of his chew, and moves his hand in a circle, signaling me to roll my window down. When I do he raises his upper lip and asks me what time it is. I look down at the blank face of my digital watch, tap it a couple times, and tell him my watch is dead. There is a clock on the case, but I would have to get out of the car and walk over to the passenger side to check it. I'm not about to waste time doing that. The guy says he thinks I'm lying about not knowing the time, so I show him the watch. "The watch is dead," I say. Then he asks how much money I have and I tell him. "Nothing." He says he knows I'm lying and I say, "Is that so?"

"We're hungry," he says. "We're driving all the way down from Elmira with no food. We want to buy some food at the store."

His partner raises a shotgun and hands it to the driver, who points it at me. "How much for your life?" he says. He turns back to his buddy, then back to me. "My friend here says ten dollars. Fair price, huh? Ten dollars and your life is yours."

I put my hand over the wallet in my pocket and thumb through the bills inside, thinking about the heart. "I don't have a dime," I say.

"Not a dime," he says.

"Not a cent."

The driver squints and releases the safety on the shotgun. "I know this isn't true," he says, closing one eye and lowering his head down next to the stock. "My friend says shoot you before someone comes along, but I'd rather have the ten dollars, so I'm waiting another couple seconds to see what happens."

I look down the double barrel, stop breathing, and I wait to see what happens. For a long time I listen to the unsteady rumble of their truck's engine like it's my own breath.

Suddenly he opens his eyes wide. "Bang," he says pulling the gun back in but leaving his eyes pointed at me. His lips move up around his teeth. "Guess you're hungrier than we are," he says, and they drive away. I fall against the steering wheel, my chest heaving, my right hand on the silver case.

Dale comes out of Ken's, trips on the steps, picks himself up, and keeps running. He climbs in the car, sucking in a mouth full of air, and says, "I couldn't get through." I throw it into drive and pull forward, knowing perfectly well what the situation is and what we have to do. "The phone lines around here are fine," Dale explains, "but Ken said the storm is worse back in Boston. Maybe the lines are down there."

"No matter," I say.

"Hey," Dale says, sitting up in his seat as if remembering an important message. "When I was on the phone, Ken looked out the window and mumbled something about your being in trouble. Anything happen?"

"It was nothing," I say. "Now in this situation, what do we do?"

"What situation?" Dale says, rubbing his forehead.

"You made the phone call and were not able to get through."

"Oh. We drive on, right?"

"You tell me."

"We drive on," Dale says, and we sit there in silence. After a few minutes a police car approaches from behind and flashes its blue lights. I pull over to the side of the road and roll down my window. The officer parks his car, pulls some papers off the dashboard, opens his door, closes it carefully, and starts walking toward us. He stops halfway, removes his cap, smooths back his gray hairs, and puts the cap back on before continuing forward. Dale looks at the floor.

"How are you this morning?" the old officer says.

"Fine, sir," I answer.

"Glad to hear it," he says. "I stopped you because old Ken gave the dispatch a ring saying you were having some trouble out in front of his store."

"It was nothing," I say.

"Ken said that some guys in a pickup—"

"Officer," I say, "I hate to interrupt, but we are on an urgent job, delivering a heart to the hospital just across town. We're coming all the way from Boston through the storm and every second counts. We have to drive on. After we deliver the package I will be happy to answer any of your questions."

"A heart, you say?" the officer rubs his head. "I've never heard of such a thing."

"Yes, sir."

"Is that what your partner has there in that case?"

"Yes it is."

"And you're taking it over to Community?"

"Yes we are."

"Then I won't hold you up."

"Thank you, officer."

"Well. I won't hold you up," he says again, staring down at me. "But please stop down at the station when you're done. We'd like a description."

"Certainly."

"Thank you," he says and backs away from the car.

I drive on, spinning the wheels a bit in the gravel and holding the pedal all the way down as the speedometer slowly climbs back up to fifty-five. After ten minutes of silence, passing swiftly over Washington Ave., down Winthrop Street, and across Thorton Ave., we swing up to the hospital and stop outside the electric doors and the lighted sign, EMERGENCY. "Here," I say, grabbing the case. "Follow me." Holding the case in front of me, I head for the doors of the emergency room. Dale takes several leaps to keep up with me. I walk right up to the glass booth where a woman behind a desk is filling out forms. Someone else, an enormous woman, sits in one of the waiting chairs with no obvious injuries. The man next to her holds a rag clamped over his bloody hand. They both stare at the opposite wall.

I tap nervously on the glass. "Can I help you?" the woman says without looking up.

"I'm here with the heart from Boston General. Here are the forms," I say, shoving them in front of her face. She takes the forms but does not look at them.

"A heart?" she says, looking at me and my metal case.

"Yes," I say.

She takes a deep breath and shifts her behind on the swivel chair. "What do you mean, you're here with a heart?"

"Look," I say. "It's an emergency. We've been delayed. There is a woman here who needs this heart. Who knows how long she will last, but I know that this heart will not last much longer." The woman stares at me, looks at the forms. "Didn't anyone tell you?" I ask.

"I just came on," she says. "I haven't heard anything about this."

I set the case down and grab onto the edge of the partition separating this woman from myself. I stare down, fixed on her lower lip. "Look," I say. "The heart is here."

"I'll have to go back and check with one of the doctors," she says, smiling faintly and disappearing down a corridor. I lean against the glass and close my eyes. I can hear the large woman in the chair shift from one hip to another. The man with the injured hand coughs briefly and then starts tapping his foot. He taps it out of boredom, not pain. Once every couple seconds he lets the toe hit the floor. Then he stops and I feel his eyes on me and the silver case. The fluorescent lights lining the ceiling buzz like insects, becoming louder with every moment until in the distance I hear the clicking heels of the receptionist and the squeaks of a doctor's rubber heels coming down the corridor. I turn around suddenly, wondering what has happened to Dale. And just as the doctor comes up behind me, I see Dale appear from around a corner and pause next to a black sign with an arrow that says *Cafeteria*. The doctor puts his hand on my shoulder and rests it there, waiting for me to turn toward him.

"I'm sorry," he says when I don't turn. "Boston General should have told you on the last call."

He removes his hand and waits patiently for me to respond. The receptionist returns to her desk and picks up the next form off the enormous stack. Dale has stopped to unwrap the rest of a sandwich he just bought down the hall. He leans over, allowing the lettuce strands to fall on the floor instead of his jacket, and then continues toward me. A sliced tomato hangs over his bottom lip. He swallows and keeps walking. After a few steps he stops to take another bite, this time scooping up the strands of lettuce with his free hand and pushing them in the corner of his mouth. The doctor picks the case up and, placing it against the wall, says a few words to the receptionist, who opens a drawer and shuffles through a bunch of papers. It is too late for Worcester, I think. When Dale sees that I am staring he stops walking and tries to swallow what's left in his mouth.

The doctor steps up beside me again carrying a clipboard. "We need to have you sign these," he says. I take the clipboard and the pen without looking at him.

"I was hungry," Dale says, shrugging his shoulders. "I figured we were here. I couldn't wait any longer."

"That's no excuse," I say and lower my head to the forms resting in my hands. I sign my name. *Time of arrival*, it says. I turn my wrist and look down at my blank watch. I look at the doctor. "Time?" I say.

He raises his naked wrist. "Forgot to wear it today." He smiles, dark circles under his eyes.

Dale shoves the rest of the sandwich into his pocket. "It's seven o'clock," he says, pursing his lips in an effort to take our job more seriously. He walks over to the silver case and picks it up. "What do we do now? I thought we were here."

I walk over to him, take the case out of his hand, and lay it down next to the wall. "It's too late," I say, but he furrows his brow and stares at the case. It is a good sign when a trainee doesn't understand how a job can fail. I remind him as we head for the door that a heart, once removed from the body, will last only twenty-four hours. There is nowhere left for us to drive. At the door he turns away from me looking for the silver case, which a nurse is carrying down a long yellow hallway. I give just a light tug on his arm, but he won't start walking until the nurse has disappeared down another corridor. I understand that this is the hardest part of the job; there is no way for me to explain how we could have driven all this way with a heart for which, in the end, there is no life.

Animal Stories

When I first heard about my mother's brain tumor, I got in my car and drove like a lunatic. I am known for erratic bursts of self-destructiveness and unpredictable lapses in concentration, which make operating a motor vehicle extremely dangerous—I get this from my mother. Any man's mother is a source of grief until she dies.

At the hospital she asks, "What is this thing?" pushing all the buttons on the remote control at once and pointing it at her nose. "It's a hat," she explains, giggling and placing it on the top of her flat, bald head. In the next bed, Sharon, the woman who overdosed on drugs, rolls her eyes. "Life is not my style," Mom says, taking the remote down and handing it to me.

I press play, but just as *The Nesting Habits of the Semi-Pulvinated Plover* comes on the screen, the doctor arrives and stands in front of us; he's come to ask how much my mother has forgotten since yesterday.

By the time this happens, it is too late for me. I already have several chins, and if I were to die tomorrow, only about four people would notice and none of them, except my mother, would be women. I'm like a nut magnet—the people I *do* know couldn't tell you what day of the week it is, and the people who want to know me look like they just escaped from somewhere. But I'm a happy man, even though this may be hard to believe given my circumstances. I lost a job (which I disliked anyway), I don't have much money (never will), and older people say I don't know anything, and maybe they're right. I once had a girlfriend who said she would marry me if I would agree to change who I am, which is like agreeing to buy a used car that just needs a new engine. Lots of strange things have happened that I don't understand. If I ever have any money, I'll hire someone to explain them to me.

When people ask what I'm doing now, I say I'm not doing much. I have interests. In 1984 I became interested in nature. You can't blame most people for not thinking, because they work instead, but now that I don't have a job and there is a tumor in my mother's head eating her memories, it's time to think about what's important in life. Lately I've been spending a lot of time shedding things, like jobs, cars, and old clothes—trying to think. It's what the trees start to consider about doing in late August—at least in this part of the world. It's when life starts to turn in on itself as if it were something that happens once.

"The tumor is fulminant," the doctor says. "We will have to perform the biopsy tonight, and then we will know the extent of its malignancy by morning." He tries to smile, turns around, his business done, and looks at the screen. "Ah," he says, "plovers."

"Not exactly," my mother says.

Sometime in 1977 God had told Mom: watch out for doctors, they just want to touch you. It was April of last year when my father, a doctor, noticed that my mother had started losing little things. Once, she came into his kitchen, sat down at the table next to him and his new wife, and said, "David, who is this woman?"

This happened shortly before she lost her boyfriend while on vacation in Nova Scotia while he was taking a nap. She left the bed-and-breakfast, drove to the nearest airport, boarded a commuter flight, and ended up in London.

"Listen," she said over the phone to me from London, "what do you think about your father and me getting divorced? I think he's seeing another woman."

"You divorced him," I said cautiously. "He's married again. I don't think about it." There was a silence, and then I asked, "Mom, what are you doing in London?"

"I'm happy, Jamie . . . I don't know," she said. "I think I want to meet the Queen."

My mother believed in God from the 7th of February, 1976, to the 10th of September, 1977. That winter we had the biggest snowstorm in twenty years, and that spring all the cows in town died of a mysterious disease. Mom used to wander the streets at night, leaving notes from God in people's mailboxes about what was important in life. "Gloves," one would say. "Fresh milk," said another. "Heat."

This is what happened. We were living in a town outside of Buffalo, New York, called Waterville, which was so free of water that during the summer people went to visit relatives in the next town just to bathe. The town was named Waterville because whoever lived there thought constantly about water.

During that summer of 1977 we were sad for each other—it was new to us then. My father moved out and my girlfriend, Alice, moved in with us. Another friend—Tom, who didn't care what happened to himself because he was overweight—also moved in. Mom spent the summer teaching us how to drink gin. We sat around the kitchen table drinking slowly, not saying much, sinking into a smaller life. We drank until what happened would not be remembered the next day.

"When the doctor comes in again, tell him I'm not going to do this biopsy thing," my mother says to me as if she is talking about a dance step.

"We have to find out," I say.

"I don't want to know," she says, "and besides, I don't have time."

Ever since Mom got to the hospital she's been thinking about what's important, and so she's decided to write a book on how animals remember. In 1979 she changed her name to Meadow Star and developed an amateur preoccupation with animals. Mom loves animals because they can't remember in the same way we do.

"The dog is an exception," she explains. "It learns from people."

Sharon, who is sprouting little clear tubes filled with liquid, reads to us from *People* magazine. "James Caan married a slut," she says. "What bullshit."

Mom pushes the button on the remote control (which I had showed her how to use) to activate one of the tapes I brought from her house: *The Threatened Pygmy Shrews* from the hills of Great Britain. Apparently, industrial fallout in the rain acts as a narcotic for the animals, causing them to become disoriented and irresponsible. Some of them wander onto roads and are killed by cars, some just fail to camouflage themselves adequately and are caught by dogs or other predators. The video shows a pale hand wrapped around the neck of a black-eyed gray rodent.

Another hand moves in to indicate parts of the animal's face. The chemical is made outside of Suffolk.

Lately, I've been trying to forget things. Mom has tried to teach me little tricks about forgetting, like trying to think about something else. But most of the time it is useless. It's like trying not to get wet while you're swimming. For all the energy spent trying to remember and record our lives, all we really seem to want is to forget. To have forgotten and not know one has forgotten, Mom tells me, is the happiness of an animal.

One of the biggest mistakes I make is trying to think about who I was by remembering the things I have done. I have consistently been much better at being other people, living out scenarios that I read about in books. My mother was the one who always said that being myself was the most important thing I could do. This was before 1977, of course, after which she became a person none of the family could recognize. But my mother's family cannot be trusted—they are all in the business of killing themselves. Sometimes people in her family do get fatal diseases, but it is usually something so intangible as to arouse suspicion.

"Do we have to keep watching this shit about rudiments?" Sharon moans.

"That's ruminants," my mother replies. "No, we don't have to watch this." She presses the fast-forward button, eager to use her new knowledge. She stops on *Animal Impostors.* A carnivore that looks like a tulip waits for insects to land on its petals before the flower snaps shut and rumbles around for a moment, masticating the captive down its gullet until opening up again, innocently smiling bright yellow.

The angler fish looks like a rock that hasn't moved for centuries, but when something edible floats by, it strikes at 1/400 of a second.

"That's a fish?" Sharon says in disbelief.

The Coiler Snake: first it looks dangerous, then it looks dead. The snake rattles its tail like a rattlesnake, but when its predator, the cat, still won't go away, it rolls over and emits the horrible smell.

The Tasmanian Devil: a thick-set, apparently ill-tempered marsupial that was once plentiful in the time of English explorers, it is rarely seen by tourists. The television camera approaches the devils at ground level. After an initial display of fear, one of the devils rushes the camera, screeching and waving its front paws in the air.

"Where's the bathroom?" my mother asks, getting up out of bed.

"You were just there twenty minutes ago," Sharon says.

"Well, will you tell me which direction I took twenty minutes ago?"

"You go down that way and turn left," Sharon says, pointing with her finger.

"Are you sure?" my mother asks.

"I promise," says Sharon.

I can understand my mother's reluctance to enter these halls without directions, so I walk with her. The hospital is a place where people lose themselves—sometimes part by part, sometimes all at once. Even the people who come out alive, maybe carrying someone else's liver or skin, look like people who have been robbed. We wander down the corridors, past humming contraptions with beeping lights, afraid that around each corner might lurk a cluster of diseases waiting to bore under our skin. There is a paralysis in hospital air. As if the air were hiding some awful secret.

If you knew me, then you would know that nothing is less

like me than the things I've done. If you met me in line at the grocery store, you might think I have been to college and that I at least could have received good grades. But my past is pocked by sores, such as an inability to spell my own name. My grade school teachers declared that I had a condition, but the symptoms varied so much that they were never able to make a diagnosis. I had a kind of roaming retardation in degenerative form. One week I stuttered uncontrollably, the next I could not tie my shoelaces. I visited speech therapy, physical therapy, and a class entitled Living Skills that taught the importance of being clean.

I was born with serious intent and not without means, but somewhere along the line I failed to acquire an adequate degree of clarity. Many potential geniuses lie like broken cars waiting for one missing part. By 1982 I stopped being in a hurry to improve my life. Shortly afterwards I stopped caring so much.

During the summer of 1977 my girlfriend, Alice, who had an IQ measured at 165, said that I reminded her of Procrustes who either stretched or sliced off the legs of travelers to fit his bed. She was the one who had to have sex three times a day to stay within commuting distance of her sanity. My mother must have known about all the sex that was going on—and that we seemed to need it like air. For my mother, cooking was as much an act of desperation as our sex. After a while we had to forbid her to use the pots and pans for fear that she would destroy the house. Tom, who had worked in a restaurant, took over the cooking for us that summer. It was just the four of us sitting around, eating mostly salads and drinking gin, listening to my mother talk about what a wonderful man she was leaving.

My father was a man of inaction; it is the most valuable thing I learned from him. He also taught me not to worry about what I am not. "You can either be you or someone else," he said. "In the end it really doesn't matter." I can't understand why he said things like that. I don't think thinking ran in his family the way it did in my mother's, though it might have. We never heard about his family except that they came from a Pennsylvania mining town where they were all miners or miners' wives. My father was a person with something inside him, an idea that had been ready to burst forth. He used to come over that summer when he left the hospital and work in his garden out back until dark. My mother sat on the second floor, smoking cigarettes, drinking and watching him bury his thoughts with the azaleas. There is nothing to replace the failure of our parents.

Whenever he encountered my mother that summer while transporting a potted plant to the backyard, my father looked at her as if she were a nice piece of jewelry he had just dropped into the ocean. She was unrecognizable with her hair dyed red and with one of her new orange or purple blouses bought from Goodwill. She was usually a little drunk. During that summer we moved as little as possible; people outside were dying of heatstroke. By about August we had more or less decamped to the cellar during the daytime, where we remained, slightly refrigerated, until the fall.

Occasionally my father joined us in the cellar for a drink, and he would talk about politics with my mother as if they were two people who hadn't been introduced. My mother wasn't sure who was President. She blames the tumor on that summer, which makes sense now. She often remarked how wonderful it was to have all these new friends. Sometimes she looked at me as if I were someone else's son.

Tumors may grow because people can't forget, as mom says in her book. A psychic friend of the family once said that my mother's soul is older than the rocks in China, which means she has a lot to forget. To me, tumors seem like illusions—they come from nowhere and steal everything. When desperate they will eat anything that we pretend to know.

Mom pauses the VCR and reaches for a drink that the nurse left for her. "What is this?" she asks, looking at me.

"It's a glass," says Sharon.

"I know, but what's in it?" she asks.

The Three-toed Sloth of Colombia: a living bug carpet—home to beetles, ticks, fleas, and a steady companion, a moth that lays its eggs in the sloth's dung. After hatching, the next generation of moths will fly, seek out sloths, and begin the cycle anew. The sloth catches its prey by curling into a form resembling a shrub where insects might choose to live.

The doctor comes in again to threaten my mother with a total loss of self-awareness followed by a painful sinking into idiocy and death, unless she undergoes the biopsy and allows him to operate. He has seen it happen to other people—they lose themselves. It is worse than death, he says. She covers her face with a *National Geographic* until he leaves.

Following the doctor, two people—a man and a woman, both dressed in black pants, black shoes, and black shirts, and with hair dyed black, setting off ghostly pale faces—sidle up to Sharon and shove a paper bag under her pillow.

"Sharon's drug dealers," Mom whispers to me.

The man fingers the tube leading into my mother's arm and comments that her body is worth about four hundred dollars in narcotics. Sharon starts slipping little pills into her mouth.

Unlike the Nuthatch and the Blue Tit, the Tree Creeper can only move in one direction, which is a serious competitive disadvantage.

Mom can't remember any of this now, but on August 27, 1977, my father cut his flowers down with the push mower, after which he never returned to the house again. He didn't see her again until last year, when she burst into his kitchen and demanded to know the identity of his new wife.

The night my father cut down the flowers my mother told me that my father was a cruel man, which is something I have never been able to see. But I learned too late that you should never trust what your parents say about each other. I think I know now that he was just demonstrating how much he could hurt himself, just for us. That was probably the most important lesson he ever taught me—that in a few seconds you could destroy days' worth of work and walk away like nothing happened, ever, as if you just stepped off a ship from another planet, everything was completely new and nothing had a name.

The things my father taught me about life have made him an unhappy man. The day before he cut down his garden, he looked up and said, "Jamie, it doesn't matter how you feel about things." Then, my hands full of potted azaleas, he said, "Do you want to end up like your mother?"

"No," I said.

"Then don't listen to what she tells you."

We stayed inside and drew the shades. The only thing that could have helped us would have been a team of highly qualified parapsychologists. That summer, if you had walked by our house, nestled between two Colonials on Woodford Road, and stood for a while looking at the peeling paint, the shutters hanging askew, and the five-foot-tall blades of grass, then you might have guessed that the people inside were experiencing some kind of sadness that was being taken very seriously. Or that there were no people at all, that the place had been abandoned for some reason. It wouldn't have been hard, though, to imagine that the three people inside were lying under the sadness of the shadows as if under a giant quilt. If you were a neighbor across the street you might have looked out your window after sundown and seen a small light at the very back of the house and asked the rest of your family if they could imagine what we could possibly be doing under that dirty light. What could possibly have happened to those people?

When my mother and I talk now it is about things like politics or migratory birds that anybody could read about in a book. This is another mistake people make about knowing each other too well; they end up talking about nothing.

The doctor comes in again and says that he must do the biopsy, or my mother must leave the hospital for the time being.

Looking at the television, I think that animals seem to get better at surviving, but this is not the case with people. We look back, we collect antiques, we go to my mother's closet when we are young, haul out her grandparents' clothes from the Jazz Age, and pretend we are Gatsbys. We pretend we are anything else, we don't eat, we grow thin and solemn, and we think about our lives.

Animals seem to have a way of seeing what's necessary and acting on that vision. When unexpected things happen to them, such as an encounter with human scientists, they look momentarily disoriented before they are at it once again—whether it be pecking through bark for worms, or, in the case of the hermit crab, skittering across the ocean floor in search of an abandoned shell suitable for a new home. Animals seem to know that whatever we lose is returned to us in time.

Normally, I'm an avid carnivore, but whenever I think of that summer when my mother started believing in reincarnation and we couldn't eat chicken, I stick to vegetables and breads—sometimes fish. Things that never had legs anyway. I think Tom and Alice spent the whole summer eating mostly celery in order to lose weight. Every day there was less of them.

That summer it felt like we were exchanging secrets, pouring them into each other's glasses and drinking them down. For instance: imagine four ways to kill yourself and Tom's mother had tried them and failed to succeed at each one of them. She had a job in the state prison system having something to do with paper which was so small that the only reason her position had not been eliminated by the state budget cuts was that only about three people knew she existed.

Once in a while we went to Goodwill to buy shorts, playing cards, or funny hats. Usually we left laughing, dressed in stripes, checks, and dotted patterns, and sauntered out to the Toyota—walking collages of other people's lives.

But our sadness that summer tasted like licorice, and my mother taught us to savor it. It was, she assured us, our only real friend, and we believed her. Sadness is not learned; it happens to us and seems unavoidable. We learn what to do with it, though. She could not have known that she was teaching us only one kind of sadness—the kind that didn't go away but whirred through our dreams like bedroom fans.

"Jamie," my mother says, dismantling the back of the remote control as if it is a mystery she is trying to get to the bottom of, "how did you do on that biology test?"

"I haven't taken a test since 1983," I tell her.

"Oh," she says, feigning comprehension. "That must have been a long time ago."

"It was," I tell her.

The doctor comes in again, his arms crossed. She tells him that she will be packing in a few minutes, and he leaves without saying a word. The end of the videotape contains short blips on different animals. A buffet: *The dark reputation of the Cormorant—also known as sea raven, shag, fish hog. Copulation occurs quickly. The pair mate frequently, ensuring the eggs are fertilized.* The camera shows a shoreline covered with hysterical black birds.

"As if that's what they're thinking," Sharon says, hands up in the air, looking at me.

When not breeding or feeding, Cormorants are often preening. A black, long-billed bird is shown plucking feathers from its side.

Mom pulls her suitcase from underneath the bed, unplugs the lamp provided by the hospital, and crams it in the lingerie compartment. She pulls her clothes out from the drawers and drops them on Sharon's lap. Sharon picks through each one, throwing the rejects onto the guest chair.

The creatures of Madagascar: the Lemur, Baki-Baki, the Malagasy Giant Jumping Rat, and the *Gastric Brooding Frog,* whose young grow in the mother's stomach for several weeks until she belches them out during optimal environmental conditions. *The Dozing Mouse—not a real mouse, but a close relative. The wild bear, followed by flies. . . . Like people, they are sometimes unpredictable.*

My mother sits next to me in the car: bald, smocked, and medicated. I'm not sure she knows where I am taking her, but she seems thankful to leave the hospital even though soon, the doctor told me, the pain will bring her back again. By that time it will probably be too late.

In the silence I start to think that the good kind of sadness is like a shooting star, which rises from within us, crosses our vision, and then sinks again. This may mean that I am hiding certain things, and I'm sure this is true. But why should that matter? I have come to love the things I do not know about my past. They are like possibilities for the future, which, to any person, is just as important to survival as food.

In a way our sadness was a kind of courage that summer, because we were able to admit our disappointment with every last thing, even if at some level we understood that our disappointment was a kind of crime against ourselves. What doesn't pass out of our lives, even if it is good, ends up killing us. Finally there is something that won't pass like a disease or a tumor that takes us out of life.

I stop in front of the house from 1977. Almost all the paint peeled off, all the shutters gone, several windows broken—it looks like an old man in captivity. I'm almost certain that my mother can't remember the dreams behind buying this house even though she still, year after year, refuses to move out.

I now remember waking up from a nap in that house on an August afternoon in 1977 and hearing my friend Tom's voice. When I went into his room to see what was happening, I ran into my mother, standing, completely naked, arms spread out, next to his bed. We were all so frozen that I thought it would take an ice pick to free us of that situation. But all it took was Alice's hand on my back for us to scatter like terrified fish into the darkest corners of what even then was a building in collapse.

"Do you remember our trip to Vienna?" she asks, turning to me with a smile. I know that neither of us has been to Vienna. "We went to the opera, didn't we?" she says. I nod. "*The Magic Flute?*"

"It was in German and I couldn't understand a thing," I add.

"But that didn't matter."

"No, it didn't," I say. My mother is in the flowering of her life: her own past has been replaced by the most pleasant memories from other people's lives. Now I have the urge to reach over and touch the side of her face before she gets out of the car, because I know she is dying. But she has darted out of the car with her suitcase and run across the street, her bald head glowing under the streetlamp. A few seconds afterwards she disappears into the darkness of the front room and a small, dirty light appears at the back of the house.

This is my entire life, everything that I remember. It seems that what we know makes us sad, and what we don't know is who we are. In the end it's all about little possibilities that vanish, like snow. My story is about what happens to sadness after it grows weary and forgets itself. There is only one sadness to speak of, and it has no name. It passes between us like air.

Thief

When my mother removed her shirt in front of third-period honors English, I was in the classroom next door taking a test. I heard her door open and saw her naked shoulder pass by the window. After that the school board fired her, and she took a job selling encyclopedias, door to door, as a way of continuing to open people's eyes to the world. In the two months she drove around the city selling *World Books,* several people who let her inside listened until "atom bomb" before asking her to leave. If they expressed any interest at all, she gave them the books and moved on. When the company demanded their material back, she refused to answer the phone for a few days. "If World Book calls, tell them I'm in Greenland doing research," she said to me while cooking dinner.

In the morning she called to me from her bedroom and tried to explain for the first time what had happened in school: "I took my shirt off in class for a reason. My students were reading *The Awakening*. Do you understand?" I nodded. She was sitting in a wicker chair before the bedroom window holding her hand, palm flat, over the open page of a book, and I was in the hall trying to look away—she had always said she could tell from my eyes if I were lying. She also said she could measure the importance of a book by running a finger along the spine. I was afraid she could see that I would become just like her. Before I could stop her, she stood, closed the door in my face, and turned the lock. I asked her to open the door, but there was no response. In a moment my father joined me in the hall, dressed except for his bare feet and the toothbrush still hanging out of his mouth. He would have to buy a pair of socks on the way to work.

At night my father washed his button-down shirt and boxer shorts in the sink, then sat on the couch in his overcoat as the dryer spun them ready for the next day. I waited around the living room. Naturally he would want to talk about the situation even though it was familiar to both of us. Every several years she would stop taking what he called her up-and-down medication. The incident would not last very long. I had known the little white pills my entire life—they had followed us on every trip; we turned around dozens of times because they were forgotten at home. The last time, a year and a half before when I was just fifteen, she had taped X's on all the windows with masking tape. I had to handle the situation alone. My sister had already left for college.

"Cracks in the windows," she had explained, but when I looked I found none. That was the summer she would sneak out of the house, when she could be sure my father was asleep, and take long walks at night in her gown and bare feet. If my father woke, he would drive her to the hospital, the last place she ever wanted to go. When I caught her slinking down the stairs one night, she laid a finger over my lips and said, "Shhh, don't tell him." I stayed up waiting for her to leave the house and followed her on foot. In the middle of an empty parking lot she collapsed. I tried to help her stand, but she was too heavy, her body loose and formless like a sack of potatoes. Some part of me wanted to see her continue walking to the Eastern Prom on the other side of town. That seemed to be her direction. She had made it a little farther every night, and I thought maybe if she made it all the way the walks would stop and I could save us both. Tears were streaming down her face. She was mumbling, but I could not understand her, so I called my father on a pay phone across the lot.

"What? Where are you?" he yelled. Every time she stopped taking her medication, my father seemed to care for her more, possibly because, like me, he felt sure he needed to save her to save himself.

He got out of bed and picked us up and brought my mother to the hospital, where they would stabilize her medication; in a few days she was home taking the pills and back to normal. Several weeks later I walked into her bedroom, where she was dressing for school. She took the pill off the dresser and dropped it into her mouth, and I asked her why she ever stopped, even for a brief time. She stood in front of the mirror and straightened her blue skirt.

"I like you the way you are now," I said.

She let her hands drop to her sides, and I regretted saying anything. In a moment she turned away from the mirror. "This isn't the way I am."

That night at dinner she leaned over the table and made my father promise he would not call the hospital or take her there again. She hated to be shut in a room and observed "like an animal."

"But we don't know what will happen—neither do you. You might hurt yourself."

"I promise I won't, but you have to promise to leave me be and don't ask why." My father and I stopped eating and stared at each other.

"I promise." My father had said it like a child; he couldn't look her in the face.

When the dryer stopped tumbling that night, my father lowered his head. "If you see her come out, make sure you grab a few of my shirts." I could tell he thought it better that she lock herself in rather than travel all over town in her pajamas. "And tomorrow leave some food outside the door when you get home from school." I stood at Mom's door for an hour or so listening for some sign of what she might be doing. Later, I found my father lying on the couch, mouth open, the day's news spread across his chest.

In physics class the next day a girl named Leslie Dawson from our lab group invited me to her house after school. Later on Leslie would become a model, but in high school no one would touch her because her face was broken out and she was taller than the boys' basketball team. At her house she leaned over me, her puffy red lips and breath filled with the lunchroom's Tater Tots inches from my face. I thanked her and backed out of the house, rushing down the street to cook for Mom.

"Mom," I said to the bedroom door after finishing with the Hamburger Helper. I thought she might not be all right, so I tried the door and it was still locked. If she was hurt we would have no idea, so I stood quietly with my ear pressed to the door, and after a few minutes I heard the flutter of a page being turned.

Leslie had told me she and her whole family would be away

that night, so I hiked the hill to her house, pulled myself up by the ledge to the half-open bathroom window, pried it open, and crawled inside. Once every several months I had crept into Mrs. Kelly's house across the street from mine, just to walk around, but this was the first time I had broken in anywhere else. It was hard for me to believe this tall girl suddenly had an interest in me, and I had to find out why. On Leslie's desk I saw a picture of a soccer player I had seen around school; in her drawer I fumbled through a pack of unsharpened pencils and two unused yellow legal pads. The tickle of the carpet sent me on tiptoes through the dark rooms. The upstairs had wall-to-wall white plush that only stopped at the cool tiles of the bathroom. A mirror covered the closet from where I chose her father's gabardine, slipping it over my shoulders and stepping back from my reflection. Mr. Dawson was larger in all ways—the middle spread out like a tent, the arms extended down to my knuckles, and the shoulders frowned.

Their Siamese strutted out of the study and yowled at me, so we went into the kitchen, where I fed him a piece of leftover chicken and a tiny bowl of milk from the fridge. When the cat finished his snack, I cleaned the bowl and put it into the cupboard.

Moonlight filtered onto the mahogany tables, and everything was silent except for the faint tick of a wall clock in the study where Mr. Dawson no doubt paid the bills and occasionally wrote briefs. I sat in his leather chair and rested my hands on his ink blotter, then dialed the separate line my parents kept in their bedroom. After four rings, Mom answered.

"Mom."

"I am reading, so I can't talk," she said and hung up.

My father still held to the idea that someday we would all be together, smiling and youthful, and he would love our mother the way he once had when they were first married. I could tell he would still do anything for her, whatever she asked. It was just that he had grown tired. He had promised when I was seven that all four of us would someday sail around the world. I had stacks of sailing magazines in my room detailing the kind of boat, ketch, or yawl we might sell the house to buy. Now it was clear this would never happen—my sister was gone from home, soon I would be gone on scholarship to college, and my father, staring out the window, was already gone in ways I could sense but not see. Each time my mother did this, there seemed less of him.

In the morning both of us were at her door. It seemed to me as long as we kept feeding her she might never come out. She had her own bathroom and hundreds of books. My father took me by the shoulder and led me away. "I don't want you to worry, hear me? She's just tired. You have to let her rest, and . . . we have to let her do what she wants." He was squeezing my face with his hands, and he was crying. I wanted to ask how I was supposed to know when she might hurt herself, when we should do something, but he turned quickly and left the house.

A bunch of fathers rolled out of their driveways as I stepped into the morning air with my backpack filled with figures and graphs. Leslie didn't understand physics the way I did. No one in our group did. I carried us all through kinetic energy.

After school I stopped by Mrs. Kelly's place. I had not broken into her house for several months. Now I needed to be there. I figured she must be shopping with her kids, so I climbed through her kitchen window and walked over the smooth oak floor on bare feet. From my front steps I had watched her hundreds of times close the doors to the Volvo, leg muscles surging beneath her stockinged leg, her fingers fumbling through the keys at the front door. The kids climbed out of the back, following behind.

The houses on the street were built at more or less the same time and in the same style, all with vinyl siding. Mrs. Kelly's house was no different. A window in the kitchen was a good try. Certain foods were always difficult to resist—cheesecake, oatmeal cookies, blueberry pie. She would never miss one cookie, even two. Or a sliver of pie. If she did miss it she would think, I must be wrong, I must be miscalculating, or she would blame her kids and say to herself when they denied it, They're lying to me again, my own children.

There was a smell inside my own house of stale air rebreathed for years. I imagined it had a texture, like skin. Everything in Mrs. Kelly's house, even the polished wood furniture, had a lemony smell. As I lay down in her bed and ran my hand over my stomach, I decided Mrs. Kelly's own skin must smell of lemon, like her sheets. I leaned over and picked up the phone and called.

"Hey, Mom."

"Hey yourself."

"What are you doing?"

"Reading about the Scythians, five hundred B.C."

"Do you know how long you're going to stay in your room?"

"I haven't considered it in those terms," she said.

"What are you going to read about next?"

"Borneo. It's warm in Borneo. When I know enough I'll come out. People walk around as if they know everything—it's not safe, Jamie. I want you to be very careful. I'll be fine again, don't you worry about me," and she hung up.

Every night Mrs. Kelly read Dickens. Her two kids, John and Sara, slept in separate bedrooms upstairs. Any pictures of the father had been removed since his departure five years ago. I read the pages she had read the previous night and ran water in the tub, sprinkling bath salts until suds appeared on the surface and white foam twirled back from the faucet. Afterward, I climbed in bed and moved my legs back and forth along the cool, smooth cotton. I closed my eyes, trying to imagine Mrs. Kelly's thoughts before sleep: her children beneath their covers, her job selling real estate, the people she knew in the neighborhood, even me walking by her house in the morning on the way to school.

On Friday Leslie called and asked what I was doing. I thought running away from her house would end things, but she acted as if nothing had happened. Possibly she liked me even more.

"Do you want to come over? We have a lot of movies on video. I'll pick you up," she announced and told me to wait on the porch. She looked tall even driving a Buick. "My father likes me driving a big car because it's safe in case of an accident." The enormous front seat was just like their leather couch at home where we settled to watch a movie on the big-screen TV. Leslie sat so close it made me sweat and she wanted to watch *Willy Wonka and the Chocolate Factory.* She had brought us each a Coke and set them on coasters, shut off the lights, and pushed play. After the Loompas disappeared and the surviving children boarded the boat with Gene Wilder for the trip down the hallucinogenic tunnel, Leslie switched off the TV, leaving us in darkness. It wasn't just the short squat Oompa Loompas that disturbed me so much but how every kid was somehow torn by greed.

"I don't like this part," she said and was quiet. "Have you ever done drugs?" she suddenly asked. "I mean, you seem like the kind of person who might have done drugs. You know what I mean? You seem cool that way. Like heroin?"

"No," I said apologetically, "nothing like that."

I hated to disappoint her, and tried to think of a comeback

lie. She was not so tall and seemed more attractive when we were both sitting.

"You don't have a lot of friends, do you?" she asked.

I didn't know how to respond so I just shrugged.

"I mean," she said, "you seem alone most of the time."

"I'm introspective," I told her.

"My brother goes to Princeton. He's introspective. He's coming home for Thanksgiving soon."

"You're dating that guy on the soccer team," I said.

"Not anymore. He's a jerk. It's not that he wasn't nice. He wasn't. It's just he thought too much of himself."

"People are born nice," I said. "So what if they stay that way?"

"You seem like underneath you might be kind of mean."

I didn't have time to reply because Mr. and Mrs. Dawson barged in the front door, sooner than expected, and flicked on the light. I was too absorbed with the perfect fit of Mr. Dawson's gabardine coat to notice the shock in his eyes. I was escorted out with a firm hand between the shoulder blades, into the car, and driven home in the Saab. He looked over but didn't say anything except to keep asking where to take me.

That night I stood outside Mrs. Kelly's dark windows and tried to imagine how her breath sounded in sleep. I climbed through the window and went down the hall to the bedroom. I could see her open mouth in the glare of the streetlight, her chest rising and falling in a steady rhythm, filling the air with an invisible cloud as I crawled beneath the bed. When her chest rose so did mine. The air from my lungs mixed with hers as I closed my eyes and fell immediately into a deep, dreamless sleep. In the morning the bed creaked and her feet swung down next to my head. I heard the pattering of the kids amidst her solid steps and the gurgling of the coffee machine, the suction of the refrigerator door opening and slapping shut. Then her feet back in the bedroom, nightgown crumpling to the floor and the hangers jingling, the heels clicking down the hall and finally the door shutting behind them. Now I knew the music and smell of her sleep. I stayed in the house all day, sitting at the kitchen table where she had eaten breakfast, soaking in her bath, reading the paper. When I heard her car in the driveway, I crawled beneath the bed again and listened for her and the children, the pots clinking in the kitchen and the news on the television reporting accidents and stock quotes. Finally she lay down in bed and reached for the book. Every few minutes she would turn a page. This happened ten times before the light went off and the springs creaked as she settled deeper into the covers. At first her breaths were shallow and tense, as if she knew someone was in the room, but then they lengthened into sleep. I crawled from beneath the bed and kneeled next to her face. Her hand twitched at her side, and I thought she would wake when her mouth moved as if to utter a phrase. I slipped my fingers into the partial fist of her hand and moved my nose closer to her neck. It had not been enough to smell her sheets and pillow, or even the breath that filled the room. She started to mumble, so I quickly climbed under the bed. In a few moments she sat up, resting there for a moment, and I could imagine her eyes scanning the room, alert for the slightest intrusion.

The next day, after listening to a lecture from my father about telling him if I was going to spend the night at a friend's house, Leslie called me. "You weren't at school yesterday."

I said I was sick and tried to sound noncommittal when she asked if I wanted to hang out, but I had trouble recognizing my own voice. From minute to minute it didn't seem like I could predict what my words would mean.

"I could come get you," she said, and I agreed.

We went a couple blocks east of my house until I suggested she drive to the Eastern Prom. It was probably the one place her father told her not to go.

"I have something to tell you," I said, not knowing what I had to tell her at all. She drove up Commercial Street and over the big hill to the prom. It was always cold there, even in summer, because winds blew directly in from the open ocean, which you could see below. Everyone knew the parking lot where we stopped was the place for drug deals. I had never been there at night. She switched off the lights and laid her hands on her thighs, still brown beneath the white skirt from a summer of lifeguarding.

"I'm a thief," I said and stepped into the cold salt air and walked to an old oak tree, where I leaned, trying to pout like James Dean. After thirty seconds or so Leslie opened her door and padded over to me, her arms wrapped tightly around her chest and her sleeves pulled over her hands. She stood beside me and studied the roots coming from the earth.

"My father said you seemed like a bad kid."

I nodded my head and pouted some more.

"What do you steal?" she asked.

"Anything."

"I thought I ought to tell you that I had sex with Frank Marsden, the guy from the soccer team. It was really boring, if you want to know."

"Is that why you broke up with him?"

"Yeah, I guess. And he was one of those guys I could tell right away I would never be in love with. Know what I mean?"

"Sure."

"Don't get the wrong idea. He's the first time. I just wanted to get it over with and not have it mean anything." She closed her eyes as I brought my lips close to hers. I could taste raspberries on her tongue as her fingernails dug into my back. She unbuttoned her sweater and shirt, then unhooked her bra and drew my hand under her breasts hanging like soft baked apples. Her breasts seemed too delicate to touch, so I found myself pulling away and running up the hill where the houses stood at the edge of the park. When I reached the road I kept running toward town. It started to rain about the time I realized there was no hurry. The cold drops soaked through my blue-jean jacket and in moments it felt like it weighed a hundred pounds.

At home I showered until my stinging feet thawed and warmed. I washed my hands and brushed my teeth to rid my skin of Leslie's touch and scrubbed my arms until the skin turned red. Standing in the kitchen, I called my mother on her bedroom line.

"I know it's late," I said.

"It's all right."

"It's been thirty-six hours since I spoke to you."

"Hmm."

"What's going to happen to me?"

She spoke in a long-syllabled whisper: "I am tired."

"I need to know."

She said, "I feel too heavy to walk across the room. I'm glad you called. I really am. I needed to speak to someone."

"Mom, I am a thief."

"I'm sorry, Jamie."

I hung up and rushed into the living room, but my father was asleep or passed out on the couch, his mouth drooping and filling the air with whiskey.

Leslie called the next afternoon while my father was at work.

"I want you to do something. Will you?" she asked, her voice trembling as if she were proposing a much larger commitment—marriage, a life together—and as if the prospect were so frightening she might change her mind any moment.

"I want you to steal something for me." She said it with the kind of urgency that convinced me a single act could change everything.

"I will."

"Something important," she insisted.

I climbed in the window at Mrs. Kelly's house and wrapped a tall white vase with painted red designs in my jacket.

"What's that?" Leslie asked when she opened the door.

"It's from Mexico," I lied, standing there with the door open behind me. She wore only a bathrobe and beneath that, I imagined, warm skin, but she pulled the robe tight as if surprised by my arrival. I leaned inside the doorway and set the vase down.

"Did you steal that?"

She had been so desperate to have me steal something for her, but now I could tell I had gone too far by doing what she wanted and she was scared. When I nodded she stepped back. "You have to go," she said, coming forward between me and the vase. She started to shut the door in my face, and I stepped onto the landing. "My parents will be home any minute. They just called. They're coming back from sailing because the weather is getting bad." With one hand she held her robe closed and with the other she pushed me gently away. Before I could think of anything to say, she had shut me out. Any one of the cars coming up the street could have been her parents, and as I walked home I watched for the Buick or the red Saab but none passed.

By the time I crawled in Mrs. Kelly's window that afternoon I had begun to doubt Leslie. I called her and let it ring four times. I knew she had been lying—the sky was still clear. I called again, letting it ring until Leslie finally answered. For the first time I realized I did not have the vase, and Mrs. Kelly would know someone had been in the house. Everything would change. I would no longer be able to sneak into her house. She would change the locks, install security, and be waiting for someone to break in.

"Why are you calling?" Leslie asked. "And where did you get this vase? What am I supposed to do with it?"

"I brought it for you. It's what you asked for."

"I didn't mean it." She started sobbing. "You have to come take it back."

I paused for a minute. "I can't. And your parents aren't there. I know they're not."

"I want you to come get this. You stole it!" she shouted, and I hung up on her. To the left of the phone stood a broom, which I grabbed and swung around Mrs. Kelly's kitchen, knocking down plates and bowls. I tore through the living room next, sweeping pictures off the wall, and vases, plants, dolls, and lamps off tables. I could see myself whirling as if in a dance, as if someone else had taken over. If I whirled fast enough, it seemed, I would spin out of my life into another.

When I stopped I leaned the broom against the couch and sat down. I picked the phone off the floor. Mom answered, but her voice sounded muffled and distant as if from deep inside a tunnel. I could tell she still hadn't taken her pills.

"I'm glad you called," she said. "I think I've read enough for now. I need to get out of this room and see the ocean. I was just about to go for a walk."

"I ruined everything," I said.

"I was going up to the Eastern Prom to see the ocean. I can't read anymore. My brain is full. Where are you? You could come with me."

"I'm over at Mrs. Kelly's."

"All right, I'll come and get you."

I wrapped myself in a quilt on the couch and thought of Mrs. Kelly. I knew the plump face of her little son, John, and how it felt to step out of the shower and tiptoe still dripping across the white plush to the closet stacked with fresh, green towels. This had been the point all along: to steal only what could be borrowed or shared without notice.

After the knock, I let Mom in, and we both sat on the couch. Mom wore the same clothes she had on the week before, and she seemed unwashed and tired, with circles under her eyes. She looked around the room, at the shattered glass and broken shards of pottery and dirt scattered from plant pots.

"I don't know what happened," I said.

"Oh well, it's just stuff. Mrs. Kelly will get over it." She shrugged.

When I looked at her she was crying. "What's wrong?" I asked.

"I don't know."

"Those pills."

"Yes, that will fix everything," she said, even though she was shaking her head.

The street darkened, the iridescent oaks falling into the gray shadows. As the room dimmed, the bay window sank into an inky black pool.

"Maybe we should get out before she comes home," I suggested.

"No." She wiped her tears on her sleeve. "That won't do any good. All we can do is wait and face her." Mrs. Kelly would come home and see her house ruined, my mother would have to take her pills again, and I would have to wait for more moods like the one that had led me to smash things with the broom.

Besides, it was too late as Mrs. Kelly's headlights shot through the front windows and struck the wall above our heads. My mother's hand tightened around my wrist. The slam of the car door and each step warned of the shock that would spread across her face. I had lain in Mrs. Kelly's bed and smelled the scent of her hair, the odor of a long night's dreamy breath from her pillowcase, enough to imagine those thousands of times she had inserted the key into the lock of the front door, turned the knob to find an empty house ready to fill with lights and warmth. Mrs. Kelly's heels stopped and her hand twisted the doorknob. As she pushed the door open, I stared with her for a second at the empty rooms, the almost-human silhouettes of the ladder-back chairs, and I felt my hand tremble with the fear that someone was waiting inside.

The Naked Running Boy

Someone broke into our house one afternoon and glued all my mother's shoes to the floor of the closet. I came home from soccer practice to find her beating a pair of pumps with a hammer. At midnight I woke and came downstairs to the kitchen for a cold piece of pizza and a ginger snap dipped in milk. In the living room, where I wandered with pizza in hand, there was someone sitting still in the dark on the center of the couch. He had short hair, I could see from the streetlight. He stood up, walked past me and out the door. I yelled after him from the front step when he had walked a safe distance away. My mother's bare feet pattered down the steps and stood by my side. She walked into the street, but he had vanished into the shadows.

The man who had broken into our house, our father, came to pick us up on the following Saturday for his court-allotted time. He sat outside in the truck with the passenger door open. My mother stood in the yard with her arms crossed, staring at him. She knew it was him breaking in at night. She thought she sometimes felt him brushing the tiny hairs standing up on her arm as she stood in the hall in the dark. Andrea and I walked around her with our backpacks and climbed up into the cab. My father drove us up the coast in silence, the speedometer climbing past sixty so that he had to jam on the brakes around the sharp corners of Route 1. He pulled into a Frosty's parking lot and popped out of the truck like a teenager except for his rough, grizzled face.

"Ice cream!" he yelled, though it was only March and still freezing outside with patches of snow in the woods by the side of the road. My sister climbed out first and walked up to the front board to read the options, her eyes hiding beneath her furrowed brow. Though she loved ice cream and our mother never let us have it, all she really wanted was her allowance, two dollars a week, another responsibility appointed to our father by the courts. She was saving money in a piggy bank so she could someday move to New York and become a dancer. She collected ballerina magazines and practiced on her own up in her bedroom because we couldn't afford the lessons. Every afternoon and evening I sat downstairs listening to her heels thump against the floor and the shrill music echo down the hall. She knew the price of a bus ticket and had calculated how many weeks until her departure. As she grew older, however, other possible expenses occurred to her, and it began to seem, at two dollars a week, that she might never make it.

"Anything you want." My father waved his arm over the breadth of the board as the teenage girl with too much makeup stared back at us from behind the counter. I ordered a milkshake and Andrea ordered a small lemon cone, costing only eighty cents. Back in the cab, he pulled a bottle of whiskey from under the seat and unscrewed the top with his thumb before taking a swig. Andrea sat in the middle, and I turned after sipping the last of my milkshake to watch her take the first bite out of the glistening, nearly melted lemon sherbet. I couldn't figure out what she had been waiting for. She ran her tongue over her lime-green lips and glanced at my father out of the corner of her eye.

"What about my allowance?" she asked.

My father's thoughts seemed so far away that he took a few moments even to glance down at her. "*That's* your allowance this week," he said.

She closed her eyes tightly and opened them again moments later to stare straight ahead for the rest of the trip while the lemon sherbet melted down her hand and onto the floor.

After we'd eaten spaghetti it was time for bed, and he ushered us to the back room with two cots and a table in between. Outside the old cabin he had inherited from his father, the wind blew fiercely and branches scraped against the panes. As always, he sat down between us on the floor with a bottle between his legs and turned off the lights to tell us the story of the Naked Running Boy. We had heard it hundreds of times before.

"No one," our father said, "not even the creator of the story, knows either why the boy is naked or why he is running." Though the details changed slightly from time to time, the essence of the story never changed, that being the boy's need to run through the woods day and night, and that somehow he had lost his clothing. I often dreamed of the white body gliding through the pines, jumping over logs, and vanishing into the swamp.

"How does he run through the swamp, you might ask?" our father said, and he answered for himself that the naked running boy jumped from log to log through the swamp. "After the swamp where does he run, you might ask? He runs through the old apple orchard down the West Point Trail and through Tarr's

Field," he explained, slurring as he spoke. "If you look out the window in the middle of the night you can see him traveling faster than any normal boy could run. The naked running boy never gets tired, and he never grows older. He runs out over the water to Damirscove Island to see his old friend, the ghost of the Coast Guard captain, and he runs around and around the island and back out over the water. He doesn't care where he runs. His feet barely touch the waves, and his white legs churn so fast that they look like a lady's white fan whirling below his white stomach.

"When I was a boy I saw him running outside this window. I took off all my clothes and sprinted out the front door into the woods. I followed the naked running boy because I could imagine nothing finer in the world than running around and around in and out of people's houses through wind and rain without sleep or food. He's out there tonight the same as when I was your age. As I ran through the night, I lost sight of him, because he runs so fast—no one runs faster. I stumbled through the pitch dark. 'Wait!' I called, but there was no answer. 'Wait!' I yelled again as I crashed into a wall of pine trees west of the house and was caught up in the sharp branches, but the naked running boy would not wait for anyone, you see. It was his curse that he could not stop running."

My father was silent then, and so were we. He passed out and started to snore. Hours went by, but I could not sleep listening to the branches against the window. Sometime in the middle of the night Andrea bolted up in bed, twisted around, and pressed her face against the glass to see what was moving out there in the woods.

After we came back from that weekend with our father, Andrea had lemon stains all over her pants.

"What is this from?" our mother barked when she walked

into the house. That night she clicked her heels back and forth over the wooden floors waiting for him to show himself, but he never would when she expected him to. In all these years Andrea and I have never spoken about what happened the next night he did sneak into the house or what happened in the following weeks in court when she told the story under the fluorescent lights. What may have happened under the cover of darkness was burned away in all our minds the moment her silken lips parted and she told the story sitting above us in the enormous room. Even I began to believe the story she told of how he undressed her and ran his fingers down her naked body.

He wandered through the house in his stocking feet. Though he bent his knees, the boards on the stairs creaked under his weight. Staring at the ceiling, I could picture his hand running along the wall, fingers tumbling lightly like a pianist's over the molding outside the door to our bedroom before he was inside, his hands glowing in the moonlight and moving toward Andrea's head. Her eyes opened and did not blink as his hand rested on her forehead. His eyes were dripping and the air filled for a brief moment with an invisible cloud of whiskey. I closed my eyes and turned away. When I turned back he was gone.

The next morning Andrea would not get out of bed. My mother yelled for her to hurry and dress as she rushed from bathroom to bedroom, water running for a moment and spurts of aerosol. Finally she burst into our room amidst sharp perfumes that twinged my nose. I sat on the edge of the bed, backpack in my lap. She darted her head quickly around, then looked at Andrea.

"He was here," our mother said. Neither Andrea nor I responded, but our mother knew she was right. She sat down on the edge of Andrea's bed and stared at the wall over my shoulder.

"Did he touch you?" she asked, turning to Andrea, whose eyes shifted briefly from the piggy bank to my mother. I thought of the white hand lowering under the moonlight, reaching the top of her head.

"Did he touch you?" my mother asked again, leaning over my sister.

My mother, who worked for the city with just these kinds of cases, had us sent to a counselor who folded his obese red fingers over a gray-flanneled knee and told me that when they asked questions all I had to do was tell the truth.

Weeks later before the case, my mother told Andrea what to say. He had come into the room and pulled back the covers. She had stood and let him run his finger inside the band of her pajamas, because he was her father, let him pull them down her body and up over her head so that she stood skinny and naked in the cool room, her body lithe and narrow, still like a boy. His cold hands rested first on her stomach. He would pause there, I suppose my mother thought, before traveling down. What I knew was confused, like a dream, and it seemed possible that I had been asleep, that the whole thing had taken place in utter silence. Andrea lowered her head before the adults and said what our mother had told her to say. It is possible that she even believed the story by then. When she was silent and it was my turn, I could not face the adult eyes. I told them I had been asleep. I didn't remember a thing.

After the hearing when the time came for my father to pick us up, we knew he was not coming, not that weekend, not ever again according to the law; still, Andrea and I sat in the front room as we normally would. When four o'clock came she ran upstairs to the bedroom and grabbed the piggy bank full of quarters, half dollars, and small bills, not enough, probably, to take a bus halfway across the state, and she threw it down the stairs. I stood at the bottom as the silver flowed like water clinking over the steps to my feet.

Today my sister and I have rented a boat and are motoring away from the shore straight out to sea toward a low, green mirage hovering above the water where our father lives on Damariscove Island. The bow slaps rather than cuts through the chop, the spray curls up into an iridescent cloud sprinkling back over us. Andrea moves from the bow to stand next to me at the console. She clutches a brass jar in both hands. We're traveling now, in a story that no one else knows, though several other people were there a month ago in the waiting room, including her husband, Jonathan, when Andrea's little boy came out bloody and pliable as rubber, not breathing. But no one else thought of the naked running boy running in circles around Damariscove Island, out over the water and back again to the island, light as fog, quick as an arrow fish.

There is nothing for Andrea to run from now. Her husband has gone back to Ohio after a month of sadness turned to fighting, maybe never to come back. Now her body is changed forever, ruined from trying again. Strands of long red hair stick to her cheeks, and she closes her eyes as we pound into the next wave.

Terns, gulls, seals, and depending on your temperament, a Coast Guard captain long dead, inhabit this flat, treeless island where the first fishermen coming from Europe lived in the fifteen hundreds, before the official settlers at Popham and Plymouth. Farm boys fallen asleep drunk in pubs on the west coast of England were kidnapped in their sleep and dragged out to sea before they woke. Rather than sail back across the Atlantic, they opted to stay on the island, fight off the Indians, and maintain camp for the next winter. Hundreds of years later a Coast Guard station was built in the protected harbor. Men in whaling boats rowed out into the waves to save sailors from ships sinking off Boothbay, Ocean Point, or Damariscove Island. My father's father was rescued as he leapt from a burning cod schooner. Andrea knows that story and the one of the Coast Guard captain who refused to leave the station when it closed. He stayed on, through the winter, and even though no one was found in the spring, people reported seeing him walking through the juniper and blueberry for the next hundred years—always at night under the moon in his dark black uniform and with his pale white hands.

When I asked, Andrea said she and Jonathan argued about whether or not to go to the movies, whether to drive across town to a piano concert on the West Side of Manhattan or stay home and listen to music or turn on the TV. She had not been able to decide, did not want to do any of them, did not want to see him. Then, it is possible, he did not want to be seen and could not bear sleeping in the same bed with her, even though it was not their fault.

A trail extends from one end of the island to the other, two miles long, and another trail half a mile long connects the north and south coasts. On the west shore sits the old Coast Guard station from where I dreamt, as a kid, the old captain would emerge like a tiny patch of fog and drift over the rough hills. The gulls and terns live there now, spreading their nests on all three floors. Though no one is supposed to spend the night, our father brought us here when we were young with a tent which we set up in the middle of the island, waiting for the old captain to wander out of his station and for the naked running boy to come bounding along the rocks.

"They won't come if you watch for them," our father said to us from inside the tent. I looked up in time to see a cloud pass in front of the moon and felt the darkness descend all around the tent, swallowing the white flash of the waves breaking against the rocks.

As we come up to the island, idling in the swells, Andrea closes her pencil-thin fingers over the barnacled green rungs of the ladder. I tie the boat off. Despite the warm weather, the island and the waters around are empty midweek this late in the summer.

Her boy's name was Henry, after the grandfather who fell in the water burning and was rescued by the captain not far from here. His pipe smoke still fills my nose when the sun bakes the rocks and moss into a pungent sweetness. I could lie down and sleep now on the rise above the old station where I stand and look back toward our grandfather's old house on the mainland. Maybe Andrea wants to walk down to the station, knowing what she will find unchanged except for the rot. Maybe she can smell the pipe smoke, too, and remember sitting on the porch in our grandparents' house eating our grandmother's baked apples from orange saucers.

In the hospital they took the little boy away once they determined he wasn't breathing and wouldn't ever breathe, all before she had a chance to see him. They took him down a white hall to a nurse who carried him farther away from the unconscious mother, her stomach slit open. Later she did see him briefly after the blood had been cleaned off, leaving him pristine and pale.

Without her husband's approval, I drove her and the boy in a plastic box across town to a place we had arranged with over the phone, an old ship captain's house three stories high facing the street with newer, flat-roofed buildings out back built without thought to decoration or history. In one of these brick extensions, the boy lay in his box waiting in line, placed there by the man in a blue suit who met us in the Victorian parlor and took my sister's check.

Two days later she picked the boy up in a heavy brass jar she had chosen herself. It was not opening the jar or even the ashen smell of the gray remains stirred by the south breeze in the parking lot, but the idea of the two days he had spent alone in back of this building in the dark box and the few minutes in the chamber amidst the hot white-and-orange flames turning blue (some of his small body would fall, yes, down to be collected and carried to us but most of him evaporated—little wisps of smoke rising so fast and whisked away by powerful fans). Because we cannot think of him without thinking of his body, we worried that he would be afraid, though of course he was no longer there.

Since 1978 when he ran into trouble on the road and had to stop driving and lost our grandfather's house, our father has lived out here, on the island, now a historic landmark, as a part-time caretaker and lobsterman, a position he obtained through guys he knows at Park Headquarters. He sleeps in a one-room shingled cabin he built at the end of the tiny harbor where he keeps his boat anchored. Throughout the winter, on calm days, he motors in with a small catch of fish, clams, or urchins from the beach to sell in East Boothbay. Guys I know with whom he once worked in Linekin Bay tell me that he has difficulty talking to them now, after eight winters alone.

Sitting atop the one grassy hill we can see clear across the horizon where tiny dots inch south in the Gulf Stream, and down upon the crumbling cedar roof of the Coast Guard station and the one-windowed shack where our father lives. I have come once a year to sit on the rock with him, and each year there seems to be less of him, more swallowed down with the whiskey. He usually listened as I talked about myself. Sometimes, because he asked, I told him one of my stories. Always he asked about Andrea, and I always told him what I knew about her life in a city so vast and complicated there was no way for me to explain.

I told Andrea that he might not last another winter. His cough, even in summer, would burst on for several minutes once started, and his yellow skin and thin limbs sat against rough wool. He refused to come ashore with me. When she asked to come with me next time after I told her about his condition, I knew she would want to ask him to come to the mainland, but he will refuse and I see no reason to force him.

I can't imagine what there is for him to do out here. He must walk trails at night, even in the snow. He talked to me one summer years ago when he was still coherent about his days taking off from aircraft carriers at night—what it felt like to catapult into darkness. It was that thrill, he supposed, that led him to it at first. Then, during the war, when he knew hundreds of people, innocent or not, were dying each time he flew, he wanted to stop so badly he was almost willing to die himself. "It was the other people," he said. "The commanders who ordered us up and told us where to fly. That was our training as soldiers, and the training of those above us all the way to the top—to do what we were told without question. Only later, after the war, did reports come out of all the missed targets, all the civilian casualties, but we knew all along. We knew every damn day."

The story of the naked running boy began with our grandfather, who told it to my father. It was my mother who later told Andrea and me that our father, a navy pilot in 1970 and '71, flying missions from an aircraft carrier in the Gulf of Tonkin, would tell himself the story his father had told him as he flew. He would picture the boy's white legs running through the dark pine forests as he lowered the nose of his F-4 Phantom into the yellow tracers rising up like shooting stars, and he punched the button dropping the liquid metal capsules that would send the world blazing orange into the sky. It was too late for him to see that; he moved too fast up over the green into the darkness.

Andrea has been standing a few feet to my left looking down at the Coast Guard station. Finally she turns and approaches me. I don't know now what she can say to bring him all the way back to his life.

She sits down next to me and opens her mouth. After a pause, she says, "I fell once, in the bathroom at three months. It seemed to take forever to land, and I thought the whole time of protecting my stomach. I think I even whispered to him: 'Hold on.' At six months one night I had too many drinks at a restaurant after promising not to drink at all, and afterwards I cried, telling myself I had killed him. 'No, no,' Jonathan repeated calmly in the cab in that voice of his like he was selling a stock. 'Don't be silly. . . .'

"And then once at seven months I should have waited for Jonathan to come home, but I took the stepladder out of the closet and climbed up to the top, reaching above to change the lightbulb. I could easily have moved a lamp in from the living room or the guest room, you know. We had oodles of lamps. And I would have been fine if I hadn't looked down when I had both my hands raised—they had warned me about getting dizzy all of a sudden. The room didn't look at all like it did the minute before. I came down and landed on my side. I held my arms out—you can see from this bruise—and the lightbulbs, both the good and the old one, came floating down after me. I must have thrown them up because I was already lying there and could see them taking their time in the air, and I wanted to reach out and catch them. I knew they would break, but I was too heavy and my arm was practically broken. I had time enough, but there was nothing I could do, and then the floor was covered with a million pieces of tiny white glass and me in my bare feet."

"No, Andrea, that had nothing to do with it. You hear me?" I say.

"That's what Jonathan said, almost exactly. That's what we argued about."

When my father flew at night, there was less chance of the gunners below being able to see, and it was easier for the pilot to see the tracers or SAMs floating up. My mother threw his letters from the carrier in the trash unread, but I picked them out and saved them in a shoe box for a time when I could read well enough to understand and picture in my mind what he was doing. One night he flew down into the yellow arrows and closed his eyes listening to the dull pounding of the shells against the hull of the plane. When he opened his eyes again, flames were pouring out of the wing. Then there was a little explosion and the Phantom started to dip and spin down into the darkness.

He pulled the handle and was propelled out and over the plane, which continued down in a yellow streak until it exploded in an orange ball. It was quiet, the guns below having ceased, and so dark that he could not distinguish the ground from the sky, feeling only a warm breeze and the sensation of falling. Without warning, the field rose beneath his feet and he rolled in the sweet smells. He had been trained, the letter said, what to do next, but there seemed no reason to move, standing there in the dark, finally on the ground instead of the steel deck of the carrier.

An orchestra of living sounds flowed out of the dense jungle he had destroyed dozens of times but never smelled or heard. The wind lifted the loosened parachute into a balloon behind him, and in moments he watched it vanish into darkness. Then he could smell the jungle burn as the wind shifted, and he saw behind him that everything was suddenly in flames. Someone from that direction ran out from the cover of the jungle covered in fire. In the middle of the orange there was a dark stick figure who did not run for long before falling down. My father turned around in the other direction. The clouds separated above and in the incandescence he could see across the field a series of heads crouching and moving toward him. In moments he, too, was crouching and running through the brush toward the edge of the jungle. From his emergency kit he smeared green paint over his pale face and wrists. He tore off his yellow and orange patches and crept through the dark with gun in hand. They tried to follow, and for two days he crept at night and hid during the day, finally reaching a river where a patrol boat picked him up out of the water. Afterwards, he flew again and again because they told him to.

"There he is," Andrea says, clutching the brass jar tightly in her lap. "He looks like a ghost." My father has come out of his cabin carrying a bucket. He doesn't know we are here.

I stand and help Andrea to her feet and we walk down the hill to the cabin. We find him standing with his back to us on a rock in front of the shack, his pants, shirt, and hands all the same discolored, oily greenish gray. Last summer he could hardly put together a sentence, so after I tried unsuccessfully to bring him home I feared he would not make it through the winter. It takes a moment for his gray eyes to wet when Andrea approaches, rests the brass jar on the rock, and stands in front of him. She forces herself, after all these years, to meet his eyes. Frail and sallow as a blade of dried grass, he opens his mouth to speak but no words come out, and I can see now that his brain is wet with the whiskey the other fishermen trade to him throughout the winter. Maybe he knows Andrea and maybe he has not seen a woman in so long. She wraps her arms around him and reaches up to his bearded face. "I'm sorry," she whispers, but he stares out over the water and doesn't understand or remember.

She steps back when she sees. "What's wrong with him?"

"We're too late." His eyes race back and forth from our faces to the water. Andrea takes his hand as I pick up the brass vase and we head up the trail to the center of the island. The sun is setting; it will be dark as we head back across the water guided by the compass toward the wavering dark shoreline. I will try to persuade him to come with us, though I doubt he will. In the middle of the island, Andrea lets go of his hand as her red hair lifts in the rising north wind. She takes the brass vase from my hand and walks off the path through the juniper and knee-high grass in the direction of the sunset. Our father raises his grimy hands to his face and rubs his eyes for a moment before turning to me.

"David," he whispers, and I move closer; he remembers that much—my name and my face, the only person to visit him each summer. He's sobbing so hard now that he covers his face with his hands. I lean over to hear what he's mumbling. "Who is she?" he asks and grabs my arm, pulling me closer and squeezing so hard I find myself tugging away. "I can't remember." He looks to where she is standing, watching us, her back to the sunset, the wind waving her long hair high up into the deep blue and over into the blank shadow where her face hides.

"It's Andrea," I say. He looks at me for a moment, searching back through his memory. "She's here with your grandson."

He squeezes his eyes, trying to think back.

"You remember, last summer we were out here playing on the beach." And I spin off a story of how much fun we had.

He walks a few steps, bends his head, and turns around. "Yes, I remember." He comes forward and places his hand on my shoulder. "Last summer." He's smiling now, relieved, his leathery chin pointing up at the sky.

Andrea takes the lid off the jar and swings the contents up into the wind. Little fragments of Henry's bones travel through the dark blue sky like distant planets before falling into the grass. The rest, no more than a handful, rises in a cloud before the burning horizon, where the wind gives his white, ashen form two legs so he can run through the air, over the island, and straight out to sea.

Head On

I was sitting in the Cluck U Chicken having a wing with my buddy Crystal. It was her birthday and she was telling me about how she ended up at the psych unit. We had just popped the rest of her Xanax and ordered a second plate of wings when she started sobbing onto her plate and eating at the same time. I suggested we take her back to the psych unit. "Not on my birthday," she pleaded and started crying even harder.

The story with Crystal is that she married a guy who used to hang her upside down by the ankles off the balcony of their sixth-floor apartment which she paid for. He was a big, angry dude whose father used to tie him up to a chair and beat him with a nightstick when he was a kid. This guy was always afraid she didn't love him enough or in the right way. They were never officially married; they had just lived together for so long that the state declared them legally partnered.

So once a month or so she'd go out with me for a little vacation from her marriage. We'd talk about running away together even though I didn't love her and she knew it. There were a lot of things I didn't even like about her. Crystal and I first met before she knew her husband when she was a doom chick in black eyeliner hanging around with a bunch of skinheads. I was a deadhead on my way to becoming a Sex Pistol at the time. When we hung around together after she was married I don't mean we went out on dates. I mean when I left my apartment, she followed me.

In the Chicken, Crystal and I were hiding from my friend Yazekevitch, who had just rolled in from Boston with a pharmacy in his hatchback. Crystal and I had made the decision to stop recreational drugs for a while and keep to the prescription kind, although we had no intention of sticking to the suggested dosage.

Seconds after she stopped crying, Crystal suggested that maybe what she needed was a job; she had done some modern dancing. That's what she called it, but I don't know what you would call it. I suggested maybe she should get her head together first. She thought maybe it worked the other way around: that you got the job and then your head came together. Both of us suspected that it didn't happen either way.

I offered to put a word in for her with the manager of the Chicken, who had, for several years, bought drugs from me until I decided to go out of business. The guy had offered me a job once, but I turned it down. Then he offered me the employee discount without the job, and I took him up on that. I was thoroughly burned out on the food gig. Jo Jo's, Barnacle Billy's, Hu Ki Lau, and the Sala Thai Restaurant and Lounge had all given me the old *we won't be seeing you later.* I was sick to death of working with people whose idea of happiness was ten thousand dollars and a Firebird.

At the time I was working for my cousin's husband at a shooting gallery at the Deering Family Fun Park across from the Mahoney Mall. Shoot the ducks, win the prize. They weren't real ducks, and the guns shot nothing but an invisible ray of light. In the afternoons I also picked up trash around the park, but I never considered myself a trash man. No more than I considered myself a killer of ducks. My friend Yazekevitch usually came down to shoot a few ducks and take a few pops from the bottle of Jack I kept behind the counter. But when I heard he was coming back from Boston, I stopped showing up to work. I knew he would drag me down. I was trying to get away from all that. I wanted a family and a future. The shooting gallery didn't feel like a place for a man who wanted either of those things. "Hit the duck, win the bear. Pay the dollar, get the gun, shoot the duck." It was an insult to my intelligence.

So in the Chicken I was talking new employment for myself—telephone sales, with the aim I wasn't even aware of at the time of convincing Crystal to marry me. Even later it made no sense—she was legally attached and she annoyed me much of the time. But in the interest of making myself out to seem like an eligible bachelor, I mentioned having a connection at the Homeless Veterans' Association who sold trash bags and lightbulbs over the phone. I really did know a guy over there. The only drawback was that we had to sell each trash bag for something like twenty dollars. Crystal raised her eyebrows. I even mentioned her and me moving in together, her being married or not. She said she didn't know whether the romantic part of our association had worn thin. "What do you mean?" I said. She told me I was using her for her Xanax. I said, "Hey, the Xanax is gone now and I'm still here. Besides, I could go to Psych and get some myself. You don't think they would take one look at me and dole it out?" She failed to see my point and kept crying.

"So I can't be using you," I said, but that really hurt her feelings, as if she didn't have anything worth using. So I tried to explain that if I were interested in using her she would be the best slut I had ever known, and she was crying even harder.

Then she lay down on the bench for a little nap, and I told her there were no more women in the world after her. I slid in next to her, and she took both my hands and made a sandwich with them. She started quaking all over, pulling my hand off my wrist. I asked her what she was afraid of, and she said she didn't know. So I told her I would stay with her forever. I would hold her hand even after we were dead, that's how reliable I was. Her eyes beamed up at me, and she asked what I thought about taking a trip somewhere. I said it was all the same to me. She started to cry again, so I took it back, saying that I had forgotten myself, that taking a trip sounded like a fine idea. I went on about having a little money stashed away (another lie) that we could use to rent a little cabin where she could sleep day and night (she always complained of being tired). She moved closer and asked when we could leave. I said anytime, right away if necessary. We could go right up there in the woods with the bears and sit under the trees. She didn't like the sound of bears, so I told her that was just a figure of speech. At most there'd be chipmunks and fish in the lake.

"A lake?" she said.

"Lakes," I said. "Rivers, ponds."

"Any people?" she wanted to know.

"No one," I said. "Just you and me." The idea frightened me but I smiled anyway.

She settled down then and put her head on my lap. "Where is this place?" she asked.

"Edgecomb," I said, thinking of a place I had seen on a map.

"Is it nearby?" she asked.

"It's far enough away," I said. "And close enough." She stopped crying and immediately fell asleep. I felt tired myself and leaned my head down on the table.

When I woke up, my friend Yazekevitch was sitting across from me eating some nuggets. He had a girl named Sally with him who didn't look older than eighteen. "How did you find me?" I wanted to know.

"This is the only place you eat for free," he said. This was true.

When Crystal woke up and saw Yazekevitch she started to cry again, leaning over her wings and mumbling something to herself about Christ. Yazekevitch and I had known each other since the fourth grade. "What's she crying for?" he asked, nodding toward Crystal.

"She's having a bad day," I said. Sally ate one of Yaz's nuggets. Yazekevitch suggested we all go down to Three Dollar Dewey's for a few beers, which sounded like a bad idea to Crystal and me, but we agreed to go anyway. In Yazekevitch's car we sang "Happy Birthday," and Crystal cried, saying she wanted a cake she was so happy. I said no problem, we would get her a cake asap. She picked up my hand and kissed each little finger. "And then we'll take that trip," she said.

"You got it, babe," I said.

At the bar I ordered a Kamikaze and Yazekevitch paid for it. The girl, Sally, who seemed eighteen, turned out to be twenty-five and the only one among us with a job. After about an hour of drinking I forgot about Crystal and Yazekevitch, and talking to Sally, started staring uncontrollably at her chest. Then Yazekevitch came back in. I didn't even know he had left, but it turned out that he and Crystal had taken a spin over to his place to have sex and pick up his stash. Crystal was missing her bra. I reached in the paper bag that Yazekevitch held out to me and took a couple of pills. I walked up to Crystal and asked how she was feeling. She gave me a huge grin. "Fine," she said, a different person in the same body. She sat down slowly and smiled at Yazekevitch.

Soon I had to take a piss. It seemed like I got to the toilet without walking there. It seemed like the thought of being there had actually taken me there. When I got back I wasn't sure if I had taken a piss or just stood in the bathroom, amazed, and then walked out again. I poked my bladder with my finger but could not feel anything. When I looked up it was raining orange drops inside the bar. Everyone seemed to be soaked with orange except for me. "I'm sorry," I said to Sally, as if the orange was my fault. She put her hand on my knee, which almost caused me to pass out. "It's cold outside," she said. I asked her if she would sleep with me, and she said, "Sure." That was the best news I had heard in a while. Then I told her I was a consultant, but I didn't tell her what for and she didn't ask. I was going to tell her that I used to work for a band, but she didn't look like she needed to be impressed. She touched my shoulder. She looked mysteriously grateful to be breathing.

I went to the bathroom again for some strange reason. I didn't have to use it. Yazekevitch followed me in with a spike, but I told him I hadn't done it in a year, that I had quit that. He told me to quit again tomorrow, an impossible task that seemed reasonable. We were in one of those stalls, both sharing the same toilet seat. I went first, releasing the strap and nodding right out. I woke up alone on the floor of the stall, thinking maybe it was the next day, but according to my watch it was only ten minutes later. I could hear the buzz from the fluorescent lights.

I found Yazekevitch and company over at the end of the bar talking to Joey. I walked over. The more I walked the further away they seemed to get, until I crashed into the wall. "Wo," Joey said. He was co-owner of Dewey's. I suggested right then that we take a ride out to the beach. I needed some fresh air. Yazekevitch and Crystal agreed. But Sally looked at me, her eyes half open, and said, "The beach?" as if sand was a new concept to her mind.

I said, "Yeah, there's a beach right down the road from here," which was also a lie. It was probably an hour away at least. Then Sally complained about the cold, so I promised to build her a fire when we got to the beach, which I knew we would never get to. Yazekevitch found his keys and we started walking out of the bar. Looking at Crystal I realized that I didn't really care whether she was dead or not. I told her that. I said, "Hey, Crystal, I really don't care if you're dead or not."

She smiled at me. "I'm not," she said.

"Yeah," I said. I was confused all of a sudden.

"I'm not," she yelled, holding her scarred arms up in the air. People on the street were staring.

Crystal and Yazekevitch climbed in the front seat. She pulled her skirt up to air things out while Yazekevitch started the car. Pretty soon everything smelled like sex. Sally had been real quiet all evening, but I thought maybe all the sex smell was making her fidgety. She didn't object when I put my hand on her. I didn't know where my hand was because I couldn't feel it, and Sally kept looking out the window. Maybe it's not on her, I thought and tried to look down. "Don't take it away," Sally said, which startled me. Had I been speaking or thinking? I began to think more of Sally as she stared out the window. She and I sitting in the back together and what I might do to her. Then I did something and she did it back. Crystal leaned over in Yazekevitch's lap and took her shirt off. Some music played but I can't remember who, and we must have been traveling 80 m.p.h. or so by fields beyond which were more fields.

I became frightened. I wasn't sure why at first. I was lying on top of Sally, my hand on one of her breasts, happy as a clam, when I thought maybe she was dead. So I kissed her and she kissed me back. Then I became afraid that I would forget to breathe and die myself, so I grabbed a bottle off the floor and started swigging out of it hoping that I would relax. I also reached into the bag full of drugs and pulled out the biggest pill I could find, about the size of my toe, put it in my mouth, and bit down. Gummy liquid spread over my tongue and inched down my throat. My tongue felt on fire; I thought it was going to fall out of my face and into Sally's mouth. I saw the whole thing happen. Sally had the bottle and was pouring it all over her face, trying to hit her mouth. I took the bottle away from her and forgot about the burning in my mouth. Pain became an idea which I could choose to dismiss, and I leaned down breathing fire into Sally's mouth. She closed her eyes.

I don't remember Yazekevitch hitting the brakes or turning the wheel, but these things must have happened. I remember Sally's face, her giant red lips and closed eyes, and I was suddenly thrown into the front seat and covered with shattered glass. We stayed like that for a while. When I could think I wondered whether my body was broken but couldn't tell. I thought maybe everyone was dead except me, but then they started talking. Except Sally.

We crawled over Sally and out the hatchback because Yazekevitch had driven the car across a lawn and head on into someone's house. More than half the car was buried in one of the rooms. Sally wasn't dead but she wasn't awake either. By the time I pulled her out she could stand against the tree, her shirt unbuttoned, breasts hanging down to her belly and her miniskirt pulled up around her waist into a band. Yazekevitch and I had our jackets on but no pants. He held the bag of drugs in his left hand. Crystal was without shirt. We all agreed that Yazekevitch had fucked up at the intersection, but when I looked back there was no intersection.

At that point I suggested we go inside the house. The front door was unlocked and no one seemed to be home. We walked into the living room, at the end of which was a bar. We sat down on the stools as Yazekevitch went around back and pulled a bottle of something out for us. He gulped down about a fourth of it and then handed it to Sally, who didn't care for any. When the bottle came my way I gulped until I needed to breathe, and then I handed it to Crystal, but she had passed out on the floor. I got off my stool, picked Crystal up, and carried her to one of the couches. I laid her down, took a blanket off some chair, and covered her up, tucking her in, brushing her hair out of her face. I promised her all kinds of things. She couldn't hear me.

All was quiet. Yazekevitch spilled the bag of pills on the bar, and we had forgotten that his car was in one of the adjacent rooms. I ate a handful of pills, swallowing them down with whatever was in the bottle, and seated myself in a La-Z-Boy. Just then Sally fell off her stool and hit the floor. The evening seemed to be winding down.

Then Yazekevitch pointed across the room at a cabinet full of what looked like old wine. He marched over there, reaching for the wine before he got there, and when he did get there he put his hand right through the glass, stumbled into the cabinet, and pulled it back without the wine in his hand. I could see a big three-inch piece of glass sticking out of his wrist. In back of the glass along the inside of his arm was a deep slit in which I could see fat tissue and muscle starting to bleed. He sat down next to the cabinet, the blood seeping out of his arm, covering his leg and the chair.

I knew that something needed to be done, and my head was suddenly clear, almost sober, but the rest of my body was paralyzed and numb. I couldn't move. Yazekevitch looked at me, his mouth open, and I looked at him, but neither of us said anything. I looked straight ahead at the staircase and concentrated on moving my body, but I couldn't. I looked at Yazekevitch again. Part of the chair and one of his legs were painted red. He squinted at his bleeding arm and used his free hand to pull the glass out. Then he reached over to his left, picked up the paper bag from the floor, and pulled it over his injured arm. I moved my mouth then but no words came out. "What do you have to cry about?" Yazekevitch said to me, then closed his eyes. I must have been crying. Crystal suddenly stood up and walked over to the bar for another drink. She sat down on one of the stools. I remember thinking: Whoever lives here must be away for the weekend. I finally passed out; it must have been for hours.

When I woke, Sally was still passed out on the floor, and Crystal was just coming down off the stool. She rested her empty glass on the table and stumbled over toward Yazekevitch. A piercing, mercury light streamed through the first-floor windows of the house, and I was reminded of how we arrived there. It had been raining and then stopped. You could tell from the mist. Crystal poked Yazekevitch in the leg with her toe. "I want to go home," she said, even though she didn't have one. She poked him again, harder this time. I could see blood on the toe of her shoe. "Get up," she said. "And drive me home." But it was too late. She turned toward me, arms out to the side. I wanted to stand up myself but couldn't. "What the hell's wrong with him?" she asked, pointing at Yazekevitch. I didn't want to say anything about that, so I shrugged. She turned around and sat back down on the stool in front of the bar. Suddenly Yazekevitch opened his eyes, which scared the shit out of me. I thought he was dead. His eyes limped around the room. He pulled the brown paper bag away from the wound.

"How's it going?" I asked.

After a couple seconds of inspecting the arm he mumbled, "I think we should go."

Crystal slid off the stool, and steadying herself with one hand against the bar, she set her drink down on a coaster. "Good idea," she said.

Crystal and Sally helped me to my feet. I could move around after a few minutes of shaking my limbs. We all stood in the front yard. "I don't feel so good," Yazekevitch said and tipped over like a tree, landing face first in the mud. He hadn't even bothered to hold his hands out or anything. I leaned over to help him onto his feet and found that most of the blood had been coming from a gash in his side, not his arm, and it was still bleeding slightly. Yazekevitch couldn't walk on his own, but once we crawled back in through the hatchback, he insisted on being the one behind the wheel.

"It's my car," he grumbled, so we let him.

The front windshield had caved in, but that was only the beginning of the problems. The front of the car pointed up at about thirty degrees and probably had its nose pressed against a living-room couch. Yazekevitch turned the key and after a deafening whine the engine started. He looked over his shoulder as if he were just going to parallel park at the grocery store.

"Now what?" Crystal complained.

Yazekevitch collapsed against the steering wheel and didn't move. Sally tugged on his shirt to see if he was still with us.

"I'm just resting for a second," he said.

Sally found the bottle of Jack, mostly full, beneath the seat. She uncorked it and took a big swig. Before she had even lowered the bottle, Yazekevitch grabbed it from her and swigged himself. The bag he was holding against his arm still had some of the pills inside, so he opened it up and spread a few in his hand before choosing three or four likely colors and swallowing them down with another swig. The bottle came back to me, and I drank half of it down. Yazekevitch turned the lights on, even though it was day, adjusted the rearview mirror, and gripped the steering wheel as if he were taking a hard corner before reaching down with one hand and flicking on the AM radio, the only thing we had.

After all that preparation he looked over his shoulder, shifted into reverse, and pressed down on the pedal. The car jolted, the wheels spun for a moment, caught on something, and finally propelled us out of the house, back across the lawn, and into the street. Something hung down and made a deafening wail as Yazekevitch shifted into forward and headed us back along the road out of town. Crystal didn't seem to care which way we were headed as long as we were moving. Yazekevitch drove with one eye closed, his head inches from the steering wheel. I closed my eyes and passed out, or possibly they were open and I had just blacked out, but when I could see again we were still driving down the same road. It was midday as we passed between long, empty fields, and I thought nothing of where we had just been or where we might be going—only of the whirling in my stomach and the insistent shaking in my hands that demanded more of everything and faster. "Faster," I yelled to Yazekevitch, and we rushed down the hill and through the next few years until each of us in our own lives would have to stop. There was no slowing down. I would have to call it resignation or exhaustion, not understanding, lying on my back in the spare bedroom of my mother's house. Yazekevitch would have to call it blind luck to land in jail for a year, Sally would move to New Mexico to become a massage therapist, and Crystal would land in the hospital half a dozen more times before finally coming to an end.

Detox

I had one last sip from my beer before I pressed my lips against Sara's neck and lost time. The next morning when I woke in the basement of the Cumberland County Detox I could still taste the salt and smell the perfume of her neck before my nose drowned in the dull odor of clothes rotting in stale sweat. My old roommate Roy slipped a glazed doughnut into my pocket for later. Nando tipped his Sox cap in my direction. The hair was mashed in a ring around his head. I couldn't believe he was still there, or there again, as it turned out, still talking about his damn Mercedes-Benz. We all knew it was a Pinto with a Mercedes symbol glued to the back.

"Nando," Roy whispered to me and raised his eyebrows. "He gets laid with that Mercedes-Benz."

"Did you see me last night?" I whispered to Roy. I had been in a blackout, and the only way to remember what happened was to go into one again. The two lives, one drunk, the other sober, would never meet, though the damage done at night would always carry over into morning.

Roy shook his head, standing in the corner smoothing his hand over an old, wrinkled double-breasted suit. Roy and I had lived together in college, less than seven years before, but I knew he was living on the street then. The last time I had seen him he had just been trying to get a bed and TV at a psych unit by lying to psychiatrists at County about symptoms, many of which were not lies but exaggerations, describing visions, voices, and suicidal impulses. They just sent him to detox, however, and detox let him out again. I tried to think of lies I would tell the police when they showed up, but it was hard to lie when the truth lay hidden in blackness. The blood on my hand and shirt and the bruised knuckles told everyone that someone had been hurt. It could have been my blood from the cut on my face. It was impossible to tell.

Roy walked over, leaned on my shoulder, and promised he would find out from Jake what had happened the previous night. Jake and Katie looked up at Roy. Jake had worked in the circus, taming elephants. His own dark skin seemed thick as a car door and the muscles beneath thick and inflexible. Katie tensed her neck, tiny veins bulging, while Jake waited for Roy to finish. He laid down his cup of coffee, leaned back in his chair, hands gripped tightly around his belly, and fixed his eyes on the pink-and-yellow-velour picture of a sailboat hanging on the opposite concrete wall. Goodwill had also donated the horrible velour Elvis, a poster of Scotland, and a faded photo of a palm tree.

Katie scooted the table under one of the dim hanging lights so she and Jake could see the checkerboard. Her hands gripped around two enormous rolls of fat that pushed at the seams of her terry-cloth shirt. Then she rested her short, stubby fingers on her brown trousers and lowered her lids, fat as slugs, over red eyes. Her yellow skin told us all that it would not be long before her liver gave out. Katie often saw the room shrink, so she preferred wide-open spaces to the basement lounge where they kept us until bedtime. When her eyes closed slowly and did not open for several seconds, it meant she was angry.

The man in white trousers came down with more doughnuts. He broke the masking tape and opened the box for us. Katie pretended not to see him, and he ignored her as she reached into the box. When his feet disappeared up the steps and the door shut behind him, we all moved slowly, one by one, in a restrained frenzy, over to the open box. Our bodies needed the sugar.

Younger than most by ten years or more, I sat around thinking I did not belong, that during the day I still ate in cafés and had a girlfriend. Many of the people around me had made these excuses once themselves. "I have been to college," I told myself and thought of the brick, ivy-covered walls. I had a job, though just working in a bookstore, and I was about to lose it. I thought about asking the people upstairs to use the phone to call my father. He was a lawyer for the city and had helped me before, but we had not spoken in six months and he had told me not to call him—not at work, not at home. I could call Sara to ask her what had happened, but I was afraid of what might have happened. She had run away from me before when I whirled through our apartment like a tornado, throwing everything against the wall. After that night I told her I would do whatever she wanted me to do. I would go away. She said she didn't want me to go away but she wanted me to stop. I promised to stop because more than anything else in the world I never wanted to see her hurt. Still, I knew I should have left. I would not be able to protect her. This time I would tell her she had to leave me, though I could not be alone.

In the basement I watched the old-timer, Jake, square off with Katie on the checkerboard. Roy came back over and said Jake had been here, in detox, the night before, but that he had heard something bad had happened down on Fore Street. He didn't know what but it was bad. Some of the others kept staring at me with eyes that wandered and leapt, always focused over my shoulder. I looked away at the ground. Sick bastards, I thought, but I was worried one of them might know something about what had happened, so I asked Roy if he could go ask around without making too much noise about it. They had all been in the same situation, and there was nothing they could or would do to me, but I didn't want them to think I was like them, as if their thinking it would make it true.

Katie suddenly stood up and yawned so widely that her tongue fell down over her bottom lip. Her fat palms reached up toward the gray, cracked ceiling. "Fuck this. It's too tight in here," she said before starting in about how a guy she knew had just walked out of detox.

"What do you mean, walked out?" Nando demanded.

"Facing three years at Cumberland County afterwards, so he just said no fucking way and walked out."

"You can't just walk out of here, Katie." Jake brushed the checkers back into the cardboard box with his fat fingers. People nodded. The cops put you in there, and they decided when to take you out. Often you got out just to arrive in jail, and this was not getting out but going further in.

"This guy did," Katie said, standing up and stretching her arms out to the side.

"Yeah," Nando barked. "Yeah, right." He shoved a doughnut down his mouth and leaned against the stone wall. "There aren't even any windows down here," he mumbled.

Katie sauntered over to the other side of the room and kicked at a metal vent. "He went right through here," she said. "Crawled right out onto the roof, jumped over the fence, and walked to the fucking bus stop."

Nando, Jake, and a few others, including Katie, were scheduled to be picked up by the police and taken to jail. I was sure to be among them even though I didn't know why. Nando turned around and stopped chewing, his eyes red, his lips powdered white.

"He must have been a small dude," Roy pointed out, then looked over at me, but I was rocking in place holding my stomach.

"Medium." Katie kicked the screen again. Everyone was looking at the spot where her foot had made a mark. "He went right through there," Katie told us. "About twenty yards down." Katie bent down on her knees, which cracked under the pressure. She had to lean on one hand. "He crawled straight down for about twenty yards, and then he went up for a while and then he was out."

Nando wiped his mouth and came over to see for himself. He bent over and pressed his eyes against the screen while Katie stood watching from above.

"No way," Nando said. "No fucking way." He went back to his chair, sat down, and turned away from the screen.

"There are ridges in the duct when it turns up," Katie said. "First you go forward. Then you hold on to those ridges and climb." Katie pulled a piece of metal out of her pocket. It looked like a part of the coffee table. She jammed the strip between the wall and the grate and pried. Finally she turned to Nando and asked if he would replace the grate when she had gone. Nando just stared at her.

"You sure you want to go up there?" he asked.

Katie stuck her head and forearms inside the duct and paused.

It seemed like she might want to turn around, but then she moved slowly forward. Her torso, her midsection, and finally her legs and the bottoms of her sneakers vanished into the black square. You could hear her squeaking along the aluminum surface and then you couldn't hear a sound. I stepped forward, believing I could follow her through the narrow tunnel to freedom. I stopped at the wall and looked in but saw only darkness.

We all eyed Nando and waited for him to replace the grate. He wiped his forehead and bent down to the grate, lifting it in both hands and putting it back on the wall. Standing back to check on his work, he noticed the metal strip Katie had used. He picked that up, too, and slipped it into his pocket.

I kept pacing like someone who had a specific problem to solve. "The problem is sincerity," I lied to myself, and practiced walking with sincerity. I suddenly stopped pacing, self-conscious about the easy sway of my hips, muscles moving smoothly over the joints. The others were watching me. "When you see her," I said to myself, "talk constantly about love without using the word." But I didn't see the use, anymore, of trying to convince Sara that I could change, so I would just call to see if she was hurt.

Roy stood cleaning the lint from his tattered suit before tapping Nando on the shoulder.

"Hey, man," Roy said. "Someone should go after her."

"She'll call back if she needs our help."

"She's facing the other way. She might be stuck and we wouldn't know."

"You go after her," Nando said, looking down at the screen.

"You let her go, man," Roy said, and Nando stood up to face him. Roy slid away and paused with his face (the jaw swollen, two teeth missing, and one of the eyes so bruised that he couldn't open it) in front of the metal can that held paper towels. He combed his hair, slicking it back with saliva. He was very concerned about his looks. The glistening, dark locks smoothed in perfect rows only to be disrupted and smoothed over again. Every few seconds he flashed a look at Nando, who still stared at the metal grate. I began to think of it, too. I tried to imagine how I would feel deep inside the building surrounded by darkness and caged on all sides, so far from human ears.

"If we don't hear from her it means she made it," Nando said. "That's what it means. Because we could hear her if she needed us." He looked at Roy, but Roy just shrugged back, didn't want to get into it anymore.

I thought of Katie running down the street. I had been in detox before, but this time was different. I looked down at my hands and asked them in my mind what they had done. If the police didn't pick me up from detox and the orderlies let me out the next day, I would walk down to Amato's on the corner of India and Court and buy a can of beer. I had hope, each time I stepped into Amato's or some bar, that a different result would follow.

I walked up to a guy named Eep, thinking I might have seen him the previous night. I knew him from being in detox before and remembered his story, that he had recently ended up in Portland from Georgia. His nails had curled up around the ends of his fingers and his eyes were bugging out of his head. All morning he had been vanishing into the bathroom to whack off. Stomach problems, he would mumble, then rush in there. The walls were so thin we could hear his short, hard breaths. After each time he would stand over in the corner by the yellow table and blink at the floor. That's where I came up to him and tapped him on the shoulder.

"Hey, man," I said. He had been staring at the wall.

"I'm thinking things out," he replied. "I'm thinking things out real hard."

"Did you see me last night, man?" I asked.

"I'm thinking things out," he said again, rubbing his hands and looking back to the wall. He was thinking in circles, I thought, and so was I. We had all been moving in a circle.

I paced the floor so hard people were getting annoyed with me. "You're becoming a nuisance to society," Roy warned me. Then he came up closer. "No one knows anything, man. Relax. It's cool."

"Last night," I said.

"No, man." He laid his hand on my shoulder. "Nothing happened last night. Nothing at all."

"If I could get out of here I would go down to Florida," Jake said, looking down at the grate where Katie had gone.

Nando looked at him and then back to the grate. "I'm going in there," he said and took out the piece of metal Katie had used. We all watched as he opened it up and crawled inside. He was bigger than Katie but thinner. He had to lengthen himself and squeeze forward. This time Jake leaned down and replaced the grate as we all stared in silence.

"If he doesn't come back, you go next." Roy nodded at me, looking from my eyes down to my hands. There were no clocks or windows, but I could tell from the shaking in my hands that several hours had passed—it must have been close to evening. My body was hungry, though my stomach was not ready to eat.

Two men came down from the ground floor. The old one, Henry, was unconscious, his ashen face slack and crumpled. Two orderlies wrapping their arms around his legs and shoulders carried him to a bed. The other one came down on his own power. He was tall and scraggly and had the eyes of a mouse. He seemed familiar, confident and relaxed as rubber, like nothing in the world could happen to him that hadn't already happened. Sitting down next to me, he placed a large paper bag at my feet and nodded his head up and down before raising a finger to part the long greasy strands of hair.

"Carl," I said. I had known Carl from Bubba's Lounge over on Bracket Street between Central and Commercial. He was there every day and then he didn't show anymore.

"Jerry," he said, moving his chair closer to mine. That wasn't my name, but I nodded anyway.

"What's happening?" I asked.

"Just fucking the dog and selling the puppies," he told me, gurgling slightly, as if there was a problem with his tongue. He fumbled around inside the paper bag, which made me nervous. You were supposed to leave all your belongings at the front desk. After struggling for a second, he pulled out a pair of women's fur boots, about size eight, and placed them on the floor in front of me.

"Fake rabbit," I said, raising my eyebrows.

"Real rabbit," he corrected me. I nodded, and he parted the hair in front of his face again, then looked at me, then at the stairs. I turned one of the boots around in my hands, going through the motions of a thorough inspection before deciding not to buy them with the money I didn't have.

"I'm sure there's someone special in your life," he said in all seriousness, "who could use these."

I shook my head and placed the boot back on the floor. "Sorry," I told him.

Carl leaned back in his chair and eyed the doughnuts, scheming, no doubt, to steal what was being freely offered.

"They'll be down to get me in the morning." Carl nodded his head and I could tell even he thought it was about time they caught up with him.

"Nando and Katie just escaped through that grate," I said. "You should go next."

Carl looked over to where I was pointing and then back at my hands. "I couldn't fit through there," he said.

"You can," I insisted.

He just shook his head.

I thought about this and had no answer.

"I saw you last night," he said, looking at the floor. "You don't remember seeing me, do you?"

"Where were you?" I asked.

"Down on Fore Street looking for a drink about two—I couldn't find one. I saw you were walking away from Dewey's. You were a mess. A total mess."

"Was I with a girl?" I whispered and looked around, not wanting anyone else to hear.

"You were cruising down the street away from this mob outside Dewey's, but no, you were alone," Carl said, and at that moment I pictured Sara's red lips, though I still couldn't remember.

The unconscious old man carried down by the orderlies when Carl arrived suddenly became conscious. "There goes Henry," Jake said. We had all seen him in this condition on the street, but out there you could always walk away. First his neck shivered, then he shook his head, and finally his hands were dancing all over his lap. Everyone grew silent listening to his fingers rattle on the chair. If there was a desire that ran deeper, that carried more meaning and nobility, than the desire for the taste of alcohol, Henry's cells had long forgotten its name, and more than anything I wanted to give it to him, even though I knew he would probably die from one sip. The craving that I knew only as a tightening in the stomach and at the back of the neck had taken on the proportions of an earthquake with him. People moved to the edge of the room as his arms and legs broke into spasms. His fingers seemed to grasp and his eyes rolled into his head. We all turned half away, watching him out of the corners of our eyes. I turned fully around and leaned my head against the wall, protected, except for the sound of the flopping, from what I thought was a horrible mistake—that I should once again be mistaken for one of these people, their arms and legs jumping away from their bodies.

He eventually stopped flopping; his eyes rolled back down and stared at the ceiling, but he did not blink. We all slowly turned around. Roy stomped up to Jake, grabbed the metal strip, pried open the grate, and eased into the black hole. For a moment it seemed he would change his mind, but then he bolted forward.

People moved their chairs back and sat down but no one bothered to replace the metal grate. A few started in with the doughnuts, but generally people seemed to have lost their appetites for the moment.

Jake stood up from his chair and paced in front of the grate. He bent over and stared down the tunnel. He was too wide to fit, and he knew it.

He turned to me, his mouth open, a question forming around his lips. Before a sound escaped, Roy backed out of the duct and stood up. Jake turned around. Nando came next, wiggling himself out in reverse and carefully replacing the grate.

"I couldn't find her." Nando shook his head. "I got stuck, couldn't move. There's no way she got by there."

"She must have," Jake stuttered. He leaned down with his mouth against the grate and called out Katie's name. His voice was hollow and metallic in the duct, becoming narrower as it traveled away and finally disappeared.

Three orderlies came down and called for us. It was nine o'clock, time to be herded up the stairs to the sleeping quarters. Nando and Jake lingered by the grate whispering Katie's name down the duct, but no answer came. The orderlies pushed them along after me. They didn't do a count because there was nowhere for us to go. I asked to use the phone and was ushered to a small booth outside the first-floor office. I dialed Sara's number and waited. My mind raced as the phone rang again and again with no answer. I hoped that somehow Carl had been wrong. Letting the receiver drop, I pressed my head against the wall. When I raised the phone to my ear again, it was still ringing, so I hung up.

We all climbed one set of stairs and another set to the third-floor bunk rooms—two large quarters, one for men, one for women. Soon after everyone had used the bathroom, an orderly came in to make sure we were all sitting on our beds. "Lights out," he announced and left us in darkness. We waited for the sound of Katie's footsteps coming up from the basement, clanging over the metal duct in the wall, but no sounds could be heard, and I lay down.

When the orderly's rubber soles stopped squeaking in the hall, Nando sat up in bed and held still, his dark outline bent over. He tiptoed over to the windows, which rose ten feet above the floor near the ceiling. Standing on the end of Jake's bed, he pulled himself up to one of the ledges and pivoted his head back and forth. All our heads turned toward him—our entire futures, Sara's too, seemed to depend on hearing Katie walking across the roof and down the fire escape on her way to freedom. I knew she would end up back in detox, but I thought if she could just make it out of the building this one time I could make it out for good.

Nando stayed up there until he had to let go from exhaustion and sink to the floor, crouching for some time, like a sprinter waiting for the start of a race. Outside, the wind breathed against the metal-grated glass. My chest felt heavy and my ears rang. I could not even hear myself breathe with the cold rain pouring downward and sideways, hitting the windows like a thousand tapping fingers. I thought of Katie trapped deep inside the building in a maze of dark tunnels. Even her cries for help would be lost in the sound of the storm. I rose out of bed and took Nando's place looking out the window. It was hard to see anything through the oily grated glass and the sheets of rain in the dark, but I imagined Katie there, sprinting down the streets on suddenly nimble legs. She would run all night into the fields beyond the city, into a smaller body with smaller desires. The skin ripped on my palms and the muscles in my fingers cramped into knots of shooting pain, but I would not let go of the ledge until I knew she was free.

The Coroner's Report

At 333 Willow Road a thirty-five-year-old woman sipping tea in her backyard falls off a picnic bench and stops breathing. A six-year-old boy in kangaroo pajamas opens the door for us when we arrive.

"You've come to the right place," he says. "Everyone is in the backyard."

Two medics and three blues stand in a semicircle around the body waiting for us. They're not allowed to touch the body until we arrive. My trainee, Andrew, removes the cap from his pen and writes: "Body supine."

"That's my mother," the boy says, his hands hanging at his side. "I called nine-one-one and no one answered so I called again and told them she was dead." He stares without blinking at the body.

"Where's your father?"

"He lives in California. We don't know where. I'll never see him again."

Andrew interviews the medics while I walk back through the house taking mental notes I will write down after we have delivered the body to the morgue. In the living room: a blank TV, smell of Pine Sol, rug recently vacuumed. In the kitchen: a half-eaten turkey sandwich, an unfinished glass of milk on a counter, a napkin folded over, the sliding glass door open to the deck and backyard. The time the boy called the dispatch: 11:42 a.m.; the time they arrived: 11:55; the time we were called: 12:10. It is now 12:20.

"Asphyxia," Andrew says, leaning down over the body's open mouth and eyes. She wears running shoes and nylon shorts, a thin gold watch, and a small silver ring.

"No purple." He nods and runs his hand along the muscles of her neck and shoulder. Rigor already, I can see from the stiffness. The morgue guys arrive in their white overalls and shortly after them Patty from Child Protective Services. The position of the bench indicates she fell directly onto the grass. Obviously no foul play, though sudden death requires we take pictures.

After Andrew finishes with the camera, he stands next to the boy on the porch. "What about him?"

I point to Patty standing by the sliding glass door in her blue slacks and tan blouse. She places a hand on the boy's shoulder and slowly turns him away from the scene to a new life none of us can anticipate.

"What happens to him?" Andrew asks. They always ask questions like this when they're right out of the academy.

"He goes with her for now."

In the back of the morgue van in the dark with the body we review the case.

"No abuse to the body, no sign of struggle, no sign of forced entry," Andrew answers my questions.

"Something happened. If she didn't choke, what happened?"

He is silent. A good sign. Above all I want him to focus.

In America the course to become a coroner lasts no more than a few weeks. When I first started there was no course. The chief coroner was appointed and he chose deputies. There was no one to learn from, no books to read on the subject, just a brief outline describing our duties, a badge, and a gun. In those days most of the guys came directly from the police, but I joined from the ambulance service, where I had grown tired of arriving too late.

The scene of a crime does not remain static for long. The blood starts to settle, the muscles stiffen into rigor mortis. Pieces of evidence, even the body itself, are often moved by inexperienced officers. After twelve hours, for instance, the temperature in the body is no longer significant. Before that time we can discover, by jabbing a needle into the liver, how long the body has been dead. Doctors report hospital deaths to us, but we do not investigate. If they do not die in the hospital or in the presence of a physician we are required to respond. A large percentage of deaths are self-inflicted. Without conclusive evidence they are labeled *natural*.

Most of the calls during the day involve accidents. A few involve suspicious death. Those calls, when they come, come at night. It is fine for other people to believe what they want, but it is important that Andrew dispense with numerous misconceptions: drowning victims do not come up three times before going down for good; a shot through the head or heart will not kill someone instantly; and exit wounds for bullets are not always larger than entrance wounds.

"One night two years ago," I tell Andrew, "a sixty-year-old man living three miles from our office picked up his coat at eight p.m. and announced to his wife that he was taking a walk. Instead, he got in his car and started driving down Route 89.

Two miles south where we found skid marks, he parked, pulled a thirty-eight out of his pocket, and drove a bullet through the middle of his head. He slumped against the steering wheel and passed out. Sometime later he woke again, started the car, and drove home. His wife met him at the door. He took off his hat and coat and handed them to her.

" 'You're bleeding,' she said.

" 'It's nothing,' he replied and climbed up the stairs for his nightly bath. He filled the tub, took his clothes off, sat down in the water, and died. We found him later. No matter how fatal the wound may seem at first, it is impossible to tell how long the person will live or what he will do in that time."

Andrew nods.

"Another man, a police officer involved in a gunfight, was shot directly through the heart before shooting his assailant dead. He reholstered his gun, walked two blocks to his cruiser, climbed inside, and died. This took him several minutes, and he did it all with no heart. You have to accept when you approach the scene that these kinds of events are possible. Another man, cut in half below the ribs by a train, lived for five hours. We arrived expecting to find him dead. He was having a lively conversation about the Boston Red Sox with the paramedics. They rushed him to the hospital, where the doctors pulled out their tubes and machines. They tied things up. There was very little bleeding by then because his blood pressure had reduced, but despite the shock he still talked to the doctors and nurses.

"We waited outside for three hours listening to his gibberish. We had found the top half of him on the other side of the switch box, where he had obviously been preparing to commit suicide. It took us an hour to collect the rest, which was spread over the two hundred yards it takes a train to stop. Despite the irrelevance of these body parts to the individual or to the investigation, we must recover all human flesh from the scene. We stood outside the emergency room with a bag filled with this man's bones, flesh, long pieces of stringy muscle, and gelatinous fat, and we waited for him to stop going on about baseball and about overhauling the engine on his Camaro. He didn't sound depressed at all. His mind rushed frantically from one topic to the next. Then he was silent. He was finally dead."

Neither Andrew nor I is a doctor and we know nothing, really, about how the body works. I am not even an expert on the ways a body fails. I am an amateur. They call us when everything has happened, and we make close observations and tentative suggestions. We observe and oversee the transportation of the body. We ask a few questions, but mostly we are the custodians of the body and all of its effects from the scene of its last moment to the doorstep of the morgue. A dead body requires us to protect its legal rights.

Later we issue a report based on our observations. Nothing we say is ever conclusive. The detectives and the medical examiners make the decision. Finally we make a much harder report to the family. Sometimes they see our badges and all we have to do is stand there with our hands crossed in front as they scream. I give the basic facts: on his motorcycle, or in a car, or crossing the street, or shot. They ask why, but they're not asking me, nor do they expect an answer just because I am wearing a badge. If necessary I will repeat the basic facts to them.

The medical examiner and later, possibly, the judge may ask our opinion, but our job does not usually require that kind of speculation, for which we are not trained. At most our observations may lead the medical examiner in the right direction. We may save him time.

Our observations are far more relevant concerning the circumstances of death. We may observe, for instance, that the fingers are tightly wrapped around the gun handle. It is impossible for a murderer to simulate what we call the cadaveric spasm of muscle at the instant of death. This can be observed before rigor mortis occurs and can help in determining suicide versus murder. The position of the body in relation to the instrument of death, marks on the clothing indicating dragging, the angle of the wound—all of these are relevant. If lividity centers on the right side but the body lies on the left, we know that someone for some reason moved the body after death. There is also a narrow stretch of time during which the skin will register a probable cause of death, either by asphyxia, purple coloring, or poisoning. One woman who appeared to die of a heart attack had been killed by a relative using a safety pin. The murderer jabbed the pin into the chest between the ribs while the woman was sleeping. Investigators later found the bloodstained pin in the same house, in the room of the dead woman's daughter.

Today my shift ends at 3:00 p.m. On Indian summer afternoons like this when the leaves have already turned and started to fall, but the air warmed by the sun feels thick and stagnant, I walk in the sand at the beach where people fish or lie on their towels looking out over the waves. My toes curl into wet grains as I push forward following the line where the wash ends and the sand is cool. People know the snow could come tomorrow or next week, so they have left work early to walk their dogs or simply lie on their backs and turn their faces up to the sun. A woman standing knee deep in the swells raises her arms up above her head. I stop and stand behind her, listening to my heart pound in my ears. She turns around and walks toward me. If I were going to introduce myself, this would be the time. Instead I lower my head and wait for her to pass by.

As soon as it dies, I think, the body begins to erase itself and return to its original elements: CO_2, H_2O. I should tell Andrew that the things I want I will not get because of the way I have to live. The same will be true for him. Our job never varies. I hope Andrew understands that. I hope he is not seeking adventure. For us, every week, every year, is the same.

At three in the morning I am reading history. I know the year the city that employs me was founded. I know the history of my profession—coroner from corona, crown, second only to the king in thirteenth-century England. I am not reading in my apartment but have come to my brother's apartment to watch him sleep. It is the only time he looks peaceful. After he has been drinking he never hears me turn the key in the lock, if he has bothered to lock the door at all. I come across town and climb the four flights up just to hear his breathing. He told me he had quit, but his apartment is a pile of empty bottles, dirty clothes, and unwashed dishes. He sleeps on the bare mattress spread across the pull-out couch. When he wakes to vomit at seven I am still sitting in his chair thinking. On top of the rug sit a few boxes of clothes and a tape recorder. The cars roar down State Street toward South Portland without interruption.

Every Monday some of the files from our office move back to the warehouse for storage. We can only hold a certain number of files current. I have Andrew carry the stack and we exit through the back of the building across the parking lot to a metal-sided structure guarded by a man in a plastic booth. He knows me, but asks for Andrew's ID. Inside, the shelves extend two stories up to the ceiling. The rows on the right contain boxes of personal effects used as current or former evidence in trial or simply unclaimed effects—wallets, watches, rings of people who did not have a next of kin or could not be identified. The rows to the left contain files of John and Jane Does going back to the time of the Portland Fire in 1891. Andrew climbs up the ladder and places the files, according to number and date, in the right slots. As we walk out our heels click against the concrete and echo throughout the metal cavern.

At ten twenty-five this morning Andrew and I are sitting in the car sipping coffee he bought across the street at Green Mountain. The smell of almonds rises in my nose and the heat steams the window, blocking my view across Fore Street to Gritty's Pub, where my brother, Brian, knows one of the bartenders.

After five days I will write a report on Andrew. We have our own way of training and determining qualification in this office. People who see a dead body for the first time may know they have made the wrong choice but not be willing to admit it. If we don't like them or feel they can't handle the job we send them back to the police, where they see us as nothing but paycheck workers. Support staff.

The best people do not become coroners. I have seen trainees turn around in the middle of the street and walk away from a body. In other, less extreme cases, the trainee forgets himself and starts to shake the body by the shoulders, shouting, "Get up!" For this reason, I am more suspicious than usual of Andrew, because he seems just out of high school—too young not to believe in saving lives, as I was when I became a medic at his age. No one that young requests the Coroner's Office unless he is hiding something from himself. He squeezes the bridge of his nose and runs his palm over his forehead and closely cropped blond hair. His red, Irish cheeks burn from the coffee's heat.

He will have to learn that the people in our office are not friends, though we are not unfriendly. We know very little about each other. Some of us live with another person, a lover, but few are married and fewer still have children. Andrew doesn't seem willing to tell me about himself. I only want to know the relevant facts. In the same way we try to avoid knowing more than necessary about the deceased. Beyond names it is only necessary to learn about the circumstances leading up to death. That the dead man beat his wife is only pertinent to us, for instance, if she may have played a role in his death. Whether or not she was justified in killing him, in self-defense, is not up to us.

We carry information. We assist in the tabulation of the facts.

"What were you doing before this? High school?" I ask. He looks eighteen, nineteen.

"Before the Police Academy," he says, "I was in the 82nd Airborne for two years. Did hundreds of jumps, all of them practice. Dozens of guys in each plane, hundreds of planes, thousands of guys all pouring into the air. The chutes popped open in hundreds of tiny explosions."

"Tell me about your coroner training. How much do you remember? How many people died last year?" It is an important question.

"In the world: 52,514,000. More people in winter, less in summer."

"How many from disease?"

"17,199,000."

"How many hearts failed?"

"11,931,000."

One person kills himself every twenty minutes in America. 30,000 a year. There are 400,000 unsuccessful attempts. 92,000 accidental deaths. 45,000 car accidents. 13,000 people fell. Poison: 8,000. Fires: 4,200. Drowning: 4,000. Suffocation: 3,000. Guns: 1,800. Gas: 700. 23,700 murders reported. 10,612 by guns. 3,043 from knives. 1,000 from blunt objects.

Sometimes, however, facts do not tell us the full story and statistics are misleading. Appearances at the scene are often misleading, too, which is why I tell Andrew to observe without drawing conclusions. I held a piece of someone's brain in my gloved hand, looked at the picture on the license of a twenty-year-old boy who had just ridden head-on into a brick wall on his motorcycle and wondered about the 7,300 days of memories thoughts and fears contained inside. His death was eventually labeled accidental, as that kind often are, though his was definitely a suicide. He was driving eighty-five miles an hour through a parking lot straight at a wall on his birthday.

In our job, timing matters just as much as accuracy. After a suspicious arson I was present during the questioning of a burn victim whose hours were numbered. His eyes burned red—even the skin on his lips was burned off. Though I stood behind the investigating officer, the burned man saw my badge and tried to raise himself up. "Get him out of the room," he mumbled through his bandages. I had come too early.

Across the street a man coming out of the bar stumbles on the bricks and catches himself on the light post. Two bigger guys follow him out and stand back. Brian turns from the light post and rushes at the stomach of the bigger man. I open the door and start out of the car but think better of it and slam it closed.

"Who's that? Do you know that guy?" Andrew asks.

"My brother."

"Shouldn't we do something?"

"There's nothing we can do."

Andrew looks at me, steps out of the car, and runs across the street. He flashes his badge at the two men, who back off and walk away. Then he helps my brother to his feet, brushes his jacket off, and pulls him by the arm toward the car. There's blood coming out of Brian's nose, but it's not broken, and his left eye is swollen shut. He turns his face away from me to hide the scar on his cheek as if I were seeing him for the first time. My beeper goes off and a call comes in over the radio. Brian steps back as Andrew lifts the beeper off his belt and looks at me. I wave him in the car. Sitting beside me, Andrew rubs his hands down over his thighs, and I can tell he won't sit still until he looks back. He does and I do, too, glancing into the rearview. Sure enough, Brian crosses the street back to the bar.

Accident on I-95, the overpass. Someone hit the guardrail, according to the dispatcher. We drive through the sudden cold downpour and blowing leaves along Forest to the on ramp and north until we reach the red and blue lights clustered at the roadside flashing into the gray midday sky. The whitecaps rise in the bay out beyond the brown stacks of the old bean factory. No brake skids on the pavement. The individual did not try to stop from driving into the guardrail, but the position of the car tells the story. The first car bounced off the rail, turned sideways to traffic, and skidded. Another car hit the passenger door and shot the person into the street, where another car dragged the person to a stop. Two other cars smashed into the first car. It could be, I think, looking at the upturned Buick Skylark, that the person was careless. It could be that the person drank too much or did not fight sleepiness. It's hard to know why it happened, though we can see from the remains and the skids what happened.

"Bottle of scotch between the seats," John Harvey, a cop from the station, says. Andrew writes it down as if the statement were fact.

"Erase that," I say to Andrew. "Write only what you observe, not what you are told."

"Two dead," Harvey says, and nods to one of the cars that crashed into the Skylark. Rescue guys have inserted the Jaws of Life to extract another man, fully conscious, out of the fourth car. A dead man lies on the ground with his face smashed in, and a woman, the wife of the man being extracted, paces back and forth behind the rescue guys holding her head. One medic tries to calm her, but she pushes him away.

Just as I expected, the body of the first person is spread out in many pieces, dragged by the second car that came along. "First it crashed against the guardrail," I say to Andrew, pointing out the twisted metal. "The door was torn off there. The car skidded sideways and rolled. Individual was pitched onto the road when that second car up ahead came along. The other body seems intact, so let's help the morgue guys collect the pieces of number one before the rain washes it away." Already the guys in white jumpsuits are combing the street and dropping pieces of flesh into plastic bags. The torso and one of the legs lie in one pile. The person's head lies where it first hit the pavement. The skin is rubbed off and the skull cracked in two. The grayish-pink contents have smeared over a distance of ten feet. The rain erodes the streak and evidence of what has happened.

"Write this down and snap it," I say. Andrew pulls out a waterproof camera and snaps the photos, jumping from one side of the pieces to the other to capture both angles. I hand Andrew a pair of rubber gloves and send him with a plastic bag in the direction of the two arms, separated from the torso and lying several feet from each other in the middle of the road. I want to see if he hesitates, but he leans down and picks them up by the wrists, dropping them in the bag one at a time. He walks back and stands in front of me, his face blank and calm.

"What else?"

"Male or female?" I ask him, pointing down at the collection of parts we have collected lying at my feet. He looks down at the bags and back to me. He opens up the bag containing the head. He closes his eyes and the bag, too.

"I can't tell."

"Check the rest."

He opens the bag with the torso, but the skin was ripped off when the body dragged underneath one of the cars.

"There's nothing left. How am I supposed to know?"

"Check the curve of the pelvic bone or the sciatic notch. Both are sticking out."

He uncovers the torso and runs the gloved hand beneath the flaps of flesh along the exposed bone, but I can tell he doesn't remember.

"It's too narrow there for a woman," I say. "You should know that a body is only ever impossible to identify for two reasons: either its remains are incomplete, without teeth, skin, or retinas, or the person was indigent and without connections. This kind of person vanishes without anyone noticing. It is rare, though, that a person like this will pass into the ground without revealing his identity. The body owned a car. Even though we have not found ID and the car has caught fire, the burned plates will reveal the owner. From there we will investigate. It is our job to identify the body, so learn to identify characteristics," I say. "This will give you the name of the body. A scar, a tattoo, dental work."

"Yes, sir."

I know how hard it is. After eight hours or less even an uninjured body ceases to resemble the person. It is much harder to identify a body that has been altered. After a fatal fire in a building, I identified the partially burned body of a friend who I knew lived there. We attached his name to the body and took him to the morgue. Two days later I saw him walking toward me along the street. He had been out of town. "Wasn't that lucky?" he said.

The woman who was pacing by the wreck has come up beside us and started to drag the charred corpse of victim number two north along the road. I rest my hand on her shoulder.

"Excuse me, ma'am. This body does not belong to you."

"Yes it does. It's my husband," she wails. Probably she thinks she is taking him to their home miles away.

"No it is not, ma'am."

"I should know my husband."

All the skin has melted tight against the bones, the face smashed in.

"Your husband is still alive. They've just taken him out of the car now, back there."

She stops, looks south to the twisted metal of the cars and the endless line of backed-up traffic. She drops the body like an old bone. The red and blue lights flash off her soaking and bruised face, and she runs.

This is why we keep family members away from the scene—they will see what they want to see, and often there is very little about the body to remind them of the person they loved. We will take it to the morgue. We have this man's ID from his pocket. Only the head and torso were burned. It is best for the family involved to hold the image of their loved one unspoiled in their memories.

This time Andrew rides in back with the body alone to the morgue while I follow behind. When he steps out I examine his face for signs of changes, but he holds the same steady expression. The color has left his cheeks, but he goes about the business of helping the guys carry the body and the bags of parts to the door. We don't follow inside because I have obtained the address of the burned man's wife, in South Portland.

"This is your first time, so when you speak to this man's wife," I say as we cross the bridge, "always restrain your tongue if you have any doubts. It is not only important to speak in a calm voice, it is important to be calm. Death does not concern the body. It concerns the survivor. She may appear anxious, distracted, she may cry, break into a frenzy, or simply be unable to move or speak. If she starts flailing her arms around, pounding her fists or screaming, wrap your arms around her, locking your fingers behind her back, and squeeze tightly. Whisper her name over and over until she calms. When you have her attention, give her a task if you have to. She can pack, if it is necessary to leave the house to visit a relative. She can call relatives. You can ask questions which may have no relevance to the case. It is critical, at this moment, for her to believe in the importance of her answer to your questions. You must frame the questions in a tone of voice that conveys urgency, as if the results of the discussion could even bring back her husband. This kind of lie has to be very subtle to be effective. The deceased's name should not be mentioned. You may ask her to recount, in detail, the previous day's activities. Look her in the eyes. If her eyes wander, ask her again until she looks back at you. Then, when she recounts beginning in the morning, interrupt her, asking for more detail, minute by minute, if possible. Pretend to write down everything she says, flipping the pages of your notebook every few minutes.

"After a short time a relative, neighbor, or caseworker will arrive, at which point you break off the conversation. Your responsibilities concerning the survivor have ended, unless that person needs to be interviewed concerning a suspicious death. Don't ever look over your shoulder as you leave the home. She may be watching you as if you were the dead person come back to life. It is important that she understand that you will not look back and that she will never see you again. You will feel the impulse, in the doorway, to turn around. You will feel responsible and empathetic, as the course manual explains, but this is not your actual responsibility."

I drive over the bridge crossing the Fore River to South Portland, where I rent an apartment. Occasionally the bridge opens when an old tanker is dragged by a tug to the giant white cylinders jutting out of filthy banks. The rents used to be cheaper on the South Portland side, but now a scrap metal yard rises on the banks across the river from the oil tanks. A giant barge floats upriver once a month, loads a pile of crushed cars and appliances, and floats back out to sea. I live on one side of the river and work on the other. It used to make a difference, passing from one city to the other, but not anymore. Blue and gray swirls of gas and white patches of foam swirl beneath us in the current. We make our way to Thorton Street, just a mile from where I live, and stop at 45, a blue vinyl-sided bungalow. A woman comes to the door. Probably Mrs. Leblanc. She guards the latch on the screen door with her hand. It is dinnertime and I can smell roast chicken. I lean over.

"I'm from the Coroner's Office, Mrs. Leblanc. May I come in?" She lets me in, and I walk into the living room. Andrew is at my side poised with his yellow legal pad.

"There's been a horrible accident and your husband is dead," Andrew says, looking right into her eyes just as I told him to.

She looks away, out the window to the drips falling down in front of the bay window and a group of kids splashing home through the puddles. Maybe she is thinking he was supposed to clean the gutters this weekend.

"Your husband is dead, ma'am," he repeats. "He was killed in a car accident."

When possible I will also report that the victim did not suffer, unless, as in this case, it is not true.

A long silence ensues as she pulls her robe tightly around her waist.

"Is there anything we can do for you? Do you want to pack, to visit relatives?" Andrew lowers the pad and takes a step as if the woman might tumble forward into his arms.

"No," she says. "No." She backs away into the darkness of the house. I lean against the screen for a moment before steering Andrew back outside.

Andrew looks back at the front of the house. "That's it?"

"Come on," I say. "We'll call Human Services from the car. She doesn't want to talk. You only talk to her if she wants to talk or appears hysterical. We have no idea what kind of relationship she had with her husband or if they even lived together. We will call it in and inform one of the neighbors."

The neighbor, a woman in her late sixties, comes to the screen door carrying her cat like a weapon. "We're from the Coroner's Office, ma'am. Your neighbor, Mrs. Leblanc, just lost her husband. We thought if—"

"Who?"

"The woman who lives next door."

"I've never met her. I don't know anything about her."

"Thank you for your time," I say.

"The woman next door lost her husband!" Andrew says.

"Who are you?" The woman backs up, lowering her head as if Andrew were threatening to hit her. I pull him away from the door by the shoulder.

"I'm very sorry to have disturbed you, Ms." She vanishes into the back of the house with her cat.

We walk to the other neighbor's house. Here we find a younger woman, in her thirties, with two children behind her playing on the living-room rug.

"I'm very sorry to hear about this," the woman says, rubbing her forehead.

"Would you mind going next door at some point to check on her? Someone from Human Services will arrive soon."

"Yes, I will. Sure. I've never met her. I don't know her. I mean, I've seen her going in and out of the house, and him, too, of course. It's a horrible thing."

Andrew doesn't take his eyes off Mrs. Leblanc's house until we have rounded the corner out of sight.

Twenty-five years ago Brian and I were sitting in a bar with our mother. His pale and still chubby fingers were spread out on the tabletop, and he looked down at his knees. I looked from him out the window where the cold rain blew sideways across the parking lot. She poured the last of the pitcher into the glass, swallowed it down, and stood up. The bartender met us at the door. He knew our mother.

"Sara. I don't think you should drive home. Not with the kids."

"Leave me alone," she said, pushing past him. I watched for him to stop Brian and me, but he didn't. Brian raced ahead, jumping over the puddles in his sneakers. I walked right through the water in my rubber boots. She had started the car by the time we climbed inside, Brian in the front, me in the back. Brian inserted a finger into a hole in the soft-top roof where the water dripped down onto the dash. Our mother pushed him back onto the seat and snapped his seat belt closed.

The bartender reappeared, tapping at the driver's-side window. She rolled it down until I could see his red dripping face turned sideways, steam pouring out from beneath his mustache.

"I'll call you a cab," he said. "I'll pay for it."

"Leave me alone," she said and shifted the car into reverse. He looked in through the window for a brief moment before stepping away. Gravel snapped up from the wheels and thumped against the rusting floor. She jammed the shifter down and thrust us forward onto the road.

In the rearview mirror I could see the tears rolling down her face—not an uncommon sight for us to see on the way back from school after a stop-off at the Grill. All the windows were fogged over except for a small circle she had cleared away with her palm. Brian stretched his hand up to my mother's cheek to clear away the drops. The crying was worse but Brian stayed put and stared straight ahead into the space cleared away by the defrost. I watched the speedometer move from fifty to sixty-five and higher. The heavy green fir trees came slowly into view, then rushed by. We reached eighty-five, approaching ninety, and I knew there was a turn ahead. We drove home this way every day. She reached over and unfastened Brian's seat belt, and this is the moment he cannot forgive.

The car would go no faster. Her eyes closed but she wasn't asleep; her lips shook. I did not see the forest flying toward us, though I felt the car leave the ground for a second. By the time I opened my eyes we were upside down, and I was hanging by the waist belt with blood dripping from my nose into my eyes. I pushed my way out through the side and stood ankle deep in the slushy snow. Brian stood nearby. Somehow he had lost his sweatpants. His skinny pale legs seemed like two small birch trees. A piece of glass had cut open his cheek when he was thrown from the car. He refused to blink, as if the world would vanish if he stopped watching it. "Flying," he would call it two weeks later. "I want to fly again."

Our mother crawled out of the car and stood, seemingly unharmed, beside Brian. She reached her hands down and rubbed his legs, and I could see blood matted on top of her head.

"Oh, honey," she said. "You lost your pants." She took his hand and all three of us walked down the side of the road in the direction of our house. Our mother began rubbing her head. She stumbled once, kept going at a slower pace, and finally stopped walking. I had just begun to believe that we might make it home, that we were strong enough to hurl ourselves into the woods at a great speed in a one-ton steel bullet and walk away unharmed. Our mother had created this illusion, and of course we believed her. She was an expert at making us believe we could continue living as we had been with little food or clothing listening in the cold at night to the sound of her throwing up in the bathroom. She stopped walking, as if someone had suddenly called her name. I even looked around to see if someone was passing by. By the time I looked back, she had lowered to her knees then tumbled on her side.

Brian never let go of her hand. He sat down next to her and stared back into the woods at the spot where we had left the road as if he were trying to remember the spot in order to return there someday. She had unhooked his seat belt—he would never forget that she had wanted him to die, too, and at that moment he seemed to stop living.

Our mother's eyes were open and her body shook. A moment later was the first time I saw an eyeball without life, fixed in the skin like a miraculous, glistening stone. I pulled on him, but Brian would not let go. He expected her to rise any moment, and he still expects it now.

There is nothing we can do for a person who is already dead. In that second they no longer exist. Without this understanding it is impossible to collect the pieces of a young woman who threw herself in front of a train and was scattered over two hundred yards and not believe that we are already in so many pieces ourselves. A hand-sized piece of skull, hairy on one side, pink and fresh on the other, is no more alive than a stone. I can drop the object in the bag, remove the glove, place my hand up to my face, and smell nothing but soap and rubber.

I came here from the ambulance service knowing about the job, but Andrew is just out of the academy, a clean kid from North Deering, the Irish neighborhood where I grew up.

Maybe, with the long shifts and off time, he hopes to have a second job as many firemen do who become carpenters and plumbers. Most of the people here don't pursue those second jobs. On their days off they like to go for long drives. To take a second job you would have to want to get ahead. This is the wrong place for that.

As a member of the ambulance service, I saw many people die in front of me. When their bodies relaxed and their eyes became still, I felt a warmth in the air that lingered for a moment before vanishing. It is not uncommon for people in that profession to develop similar superstitions. Sometimes for weeks after this kind of event I would be violently sick with what felt like the flu, and I began to imagine in the midst of fever that the dead person's spirit was inside me struggling for life. In the ambulance service I learned that there was little I could do to save someone, and in this job I have learned that there is nothing I can do to bring someone back.

Andrew sips from his coffee as we wait for a call. I know he's still thinking about the woman we visited yesterday to report her husband's death. "When they finally do believe you, they will remember your eyes and your unwavering, monotone voice. They won't believe it because it's true, they will believe you because of the way you told them. Sometimes these people will find your name and phone number. They will call you at home to scream at you. Remember that you are not to blame. These people calling in the middle of the night no longer deserve or require your attention. If statistics are true and eight out of ten cases are accidental, then they are calling you because there is no one to blame."

As we are leaving the office, the secretary gives Andrew a message. He reads it by the door and walks back over to his desk to pick up the phone.

"Who's it from?" I ask.

He pretends not to hear me.

"Who's it from?"

He stops dialing and hands me the note, saying the woman from yesterday whose husband died called and wanted to speak to him.

"You don't speak to her," I say. "Your job is completed. You brought her the information. That does not make you responsible for her later. It cannot become your problem if she has no other people to whom she can turn. You are a stranger. Do you understand?"

He nods as we walk out to the car. Ten minutes later a call comes in on the cellular.

"Who is it?" he asks. "All right. Put her through." Andrew closes his eyes and listens as the person speaks. "How did you get this number? That's all I know. I have to go." He hangs up with the voice still pouring out of the receiver.

"Who was that?" I ask. "Her?"

He just shakes his head.

As we pass up Congress Street, Brian's standing outside the AA meeting slightly apart from the others in his green polo shirt and basketball sneakers. He doesn't want to talk to them and they have given up on him. I know from when I quit myself that if you go back to drinking too many times the AA people stop talking to you. One guy walks a wide circle around him just to avoid getting near him, as if Brian's bad luck could be transmitted through the air. He steps off the curb and looks both ways to see if I'm coming. He cups his hands together in the golf grip familiar to his year and a half on the college team, raises them above his head, and swings through. His hips and shoulders twist and his head looks up. You might think he had just come from the golf course if not for the black eyes and stitched chin.

"Where are we going to take him?" Andrew asks.

"Just down the road. He's staying at a halfway house."

Brian opens the door and climbs in the backseat. Andrew turns around and offers his hand.

Brian's square jaw seems to hang loosely by threads. He nods and stares past Andrew to the road, the red light, and the people in suits crossing the street to Fleet Bank.

"You used to play golf," Andrew says, rubbing his chin nervously.

Brian's eyes flicker for a moment in Andrew's direction, but he doesn't seem to hear. I've been watching him in the rearview mirror, but I'm driving now, climbing up Commercial Street. When I stop, Brian gets out of the car and doesn't look back to wave.

"Your brother doesn't want to answer any of my questions."

"Maybe he didn't hear you."

"Is there something wrong with his hearing?"

"I don't know."

He walks across the pavement with a slight limp. The heat from the sun rises in waves around his legs so that he seems to float—the shirt and pants, even his arms seem to waver in ripples.

"Should we let him go like that?" Andrew asks, staring out the window.

Even if there was enough of him to bring back, he would soon slip between our fingers like water cupped in the hand. If Andrew doesn't see that already, there's no way I can make him see. Brian may show up on my doorstep tonight and he may keep walking to the back of the halfway house, to the edge of town, never to be seen again. He has vanished before.

It is partially my responsibility to ascertain if the trainee remembers the necessary information. In some remote areas where skills have not been passed on, the coroner has no guidelines for handling the death or the surviving family. Sometimes families find out through the press. Sometimes murder victims are cremated before their bodies are examined, and quite often deaths are not reported to the coroner at all. Bodies may even be wrongly identified and buried under false names.

To prevent this from happening I must decide if the trainee is capable of the job. He has no idea, during this period, that an evaluation is taking place. Now that the course is over, he believes the job is secure by right and qualification. I am taking a left on Forest Avenue now, driving by the giant yellow-and-orange McDonald's sign. Andrew's face turns orange in the glow as he looks toward the people still inside mopping the floors.

"Can you tell me the seventeen kinds of deaths that must be reported to the coroner?"

The next generation of police, nurses, doctors, and morticians may not receive this information from their superiors. It is the coroner's job to periodically inform them, and it will become his job when I am gone to inform the coroners who train under him.

He closes his eyes and points his face forward. This may be one of the easiest questions.

"Homicide or suicide?" he says with his eyes still closed. "Accident or injury. Suspicion of criminal act. No physician in attendance."

"You rearranged the order."

"Medical attendance less than twenty-four hours of death."

"That's enough for now."

"I thought those middle three should go at the end. They seemed less significant."

"Once the person is dead, there is no gradation."

I pull into the McDonald's and park. He gets out, crosses to the door of the restaurant, and steps back. I hold the door open for him. Inside, the lights blind him. I squint, but he closes his eyes, bends his head, and raises his forearm as if to block a punch. At the counter I order coffee and a Danish. He has walked to the far corner of the room and leaned against the dark window.

"I'm not hungry."

"What happened to you?" I ask.

Maybe he remembers something that happened, maybe something happened he can't remember, and maybe he remembers something that never happened. It hardly matters which.

"Nothing," he says.

"What is wrong?"

"I don't know. I don't know."

A call comes in on the beeper. Suspicious death on the Eastern Prom, the dispatcher tells us in the car.

"What time is it?" I ask as we step out on Bryant Street.

"Nine-fifteen."

"Don't tell me. Write it down. " He takes out his notebook and marks the time.

Only investigating officers have arrived. I let him go first so I can watch his approach. Our first priority is the body, but not at the expense of the scene. Signs of the criminal's path, if there was a criminal, must not be disturbed. We do not touch the door, nor walk through the middle of the passageway, nor the middle of the room. The alleged assailant may have walked through the middle of the room to where the woman sits in a chair with a gaping wound in her neck exposing the esophagus.

"Putrefaction?"

"Not yet."

"Temperature?"

He takes the needle out of the case, lifts the woman's shirt, locates her liver, and jabs into the skin.

"Ten degrees."

"More than an hour."

He cups his hands gently under the woman's jaw and moves it back and forth. Her entire head, fixed eyes, and filthy brown hair move also.

"Rigor," he says and notes on his pad. "More than three hours." He moves his hand along the muscle of her neck to test the muscle tension there. "Less than five."

The woman's mouth is open, the tongue stuck out. Common.

The investigating officer has found the woman's purse and ID. Kathleen Danby, aged forty-three. These items go in a small plastic bag.

"Throat cut on left side—three inches," Andrew says. "Knife sits in her lap next to left hand. No bleeding at the throat. Cut after she was dead."

He looks at me.

"What about the hand?"

He looks from the hand to me and back to the hand.

"The knife sits next to the wrong hand."

"And the neck?"

"No hesitation marks. A straight cut. No angle. And no cadaveric spasm in the hand. The hand muscles would still be gripping the knife."

He jumps up suddenly and steps back from the body. His eyes race over the face and neck.

"Coloring?" I ask.

"Normal. She didn't die from the knife wound."

"What haven't you checked?"

He steps forward and carefully removes her shirt. Her back and shoulders have turned bluish purple where the blood has settled. Lividity on the back. She was moved, sometime after death, to the chair from the floor. The detectives discover a blood spot on the floor suggesting this. Andrew checks her head.

"She was shot. Entrance wound, more than two feet away, three centimeter diameter. Slightly concave. Exit four centimeters, back right. Minor bleeding. Instant death."

"Tweezer the fibers, photo, and bag the hands."

Andrew removes the tweezers from the case, collects several fibers, and wraps paper bags around the hands to protect them. The ME will want to check the nails later. The morgue guys arrive. They stand in the corner in their white overalls with their stretcher and body bag. Andrew stands on a chair above the woman photographing. He moves five feet back, shoots, five feet to the side, shoots. He hands me the plastic bag of fibers. The morgue guys step forward to bag the body. Andrew's eyes watch their every move.

"Be careful of the hands," he says.

One of the morgue guys I have known for years scratches his chin and looks from him to me. It's a new guy, he knows. Nothing worth mentioning. Andrew is correct, though. He accurately recalls his instruction. From this point until we reach the morgue, in a suspicious death like this, our eyes cannot leave the body. We will both ride in the back of the van in the dark with the body. The morgue guys ride up front. Two benches have been provided in the back for this purpose. The gurney is secured in the middle between us. Before they close the doors I can see Andrew's eyes illuminated by the streetlights staring down at the bulge of the woman's head against the black plastic. Then we are in complete darkness. No windows. The van bounces along Commercial, down the hill to the "butcher shop," we call it. I know the sound of every street in this town. Some of the potholes on this hill haven't been filled since I learned how to drive. We rise slightly before continuing down.

Now at sea level on cobblestone by the empty warehouse, and into the underground garage. Fluorescent lights burn as the doors swing open. Andrew's eyes haven't moved from the body the entire time, even in darkness.

"Come on," I say. "Let them work."

He backs off and we follow the gurney down a gentle slope to a pair of electric-eye doors. These are not the significant doors. The important doors come next. They are blue and can only be opened with the card the morgue guys carry in their pockets. Beyond these doors the body is technically now in the jurisdiction of the medical examiner, but we follow down the plain white hall, no windows, still descending. We turn right at the bottom. The building goes no deeper than two stories. There at the desk we sign our names. The morgue guys sign their names. Another man appears from a door behind the counter. The woman sitting at the desk never looks up. The man who has just appeared will take the gurney the rest of the way down the hall to the morgue. The others are friendly. The morgue guys will drive us back to our car, but Andrew won't turn around. He watches the body roll down the hall to the silver metal doors twenty yards away.

"Andrew," I say. "We're done."

"Are we allowed to follow?"

"There is no reason for us to. The body is their responsibility."

"Are we allowed?"

"You are asking the wrong question," I say. The gurney pushes through the metal doors and both the body and the attendant in white vanish down the white hall.

At the scene the investigating team has taken over. They will search every inch, find the bullet, and probably find the assailant. Eighty percent of murders are committed by the victim's relations. Her ex-husband, an ex-felon, will be one of the first people paid a visit. He will be the right person. Nothing in the room was taken. We found her purse, containing $150 and a gram of heroin. This crime, like most, was committed for more complicated reasons than theft.

The blue lights flash across Andrew's face; his eyes race over the building as if expecting to find the clues written on the clapboards.

"Now we go back to the office and write our reports. We may write brief conjectural recommendations at the end, but our duty is to report what we observed, nothing more."

Andrew purses his lips and closes his eyes, lowering his head. "Don't we have to do something to find out who did that?"

"No, we don't," I say. "That's not our job."

In the car he leans forward and holds his stomach.

"Are you all right?"

"I'll be fine."

But I pull the car over. "You tell me what it is," I demand.

"It's just that it happened so recently," he says. "A friend I grew up with next door. He and I joined the army together after high school. He was behind me on the line during a day jump when something went wrong. His chute didn't open. He reached out his hand as he passed by. I could see his eyes as if he had paused in the air. I tried to get loose from my chute. I wanted to go after him. I found him on the ground. He was pressed into the dirt, his body limp like a sack of sand. No matter how much the CO yelled at me, I couldn't get up. They had to carry me out of the field. It happened during the end of my time. We were about to sign up for another hitch. What gets me is that he had time to think as he fell. I can't stop wondering what went through his mind as he fell. I watched him fall all the way. It was a clear, bright day. He shrank to the size of a tiny dot before hitting the ground."

I start the car again and continue driving.

After our shift I wait outside in the parking lot for Andrew to climb on his motorcycle. No doubt the woman gave him a call this afternoon because she had nowhere else to turn. She remembered his face, and he says to himself that he will just stop by to see if she is safe. I know what he is going to do. He looks at his watch, pulls the helmet down, and heads out up State Street and left down the hill and across the bridge to South Portland to Thorton Street, the home of the woman who lost her husband. He pauses for a minute as he steps off the bike. I have parked down the street in a shadow. Hopefully, he considers what he has learned in the manual or what I might say. He tucks his helmet under his arm and walks up to the door.

She has been waiting for him. She comes out onto the landing and wraps her arms around his chest—not as a lover, around his neck, but as a child. She sobs and rests her weight on him. He drops the helmet in order to hold her up. She has moved her hands inside his shirt and closed her eyes. She's not with him anymore but with her husband who no longer exists. He thinks he's in love with her, but he's just become a ghost. She presses her lips against his, and he hopes she will bring him back to life. This struggle not to vanish is what takes him inside the house, where he removes his clothes in the front room to press his skin against hers, to feel her heat. I know what it is like to want that.

My mother used to run across the lawn as if she did not know what to do with her hands. They would hang at her side like leaden wings. Brian would follow her, his arms raised in the air. He imagined himself a winged fighter pilot protecting her.

A year after the accident I found him on the second floor of our grandparents' house in his Superman cape crouching in the window, ready to leap. I should have grabbed him from behind.

I should have run across the room screaming his name. Instead I just spoke. He heard me, and turned his head. I saw the Magic Marker S on the cape and walked easily across the room to sit down on the edge of the bed. I knew there was a fence and metal stakes just below the window in the yard.

He never looked down but up toward the seagulls and the tips of pine trees.

"I am," he said.

"What?"

"I am. I am. I am!" he screamed.

I lunged forward, grabbing him around the waist, hauling him to the floor, burying my head against his chest and squeezing as he beat his fists on my back, still screaming. I have always known when he was about to jump, and I imagine I can feel what he feels falling to the ground in the middle of the night after someone has hit him halfway across town from my apartment.

Years later I waited up at night staring at the ceiling. Sometimes he would not come home at all and I would see the sun rise in the window. Other times he came home with his feet stumbling on the porch. Only my grandfather was alive then, and he was too old to do anything. I rushed downstairs to the front porch, where he was either passed out or trying to find his keys. I put my hands in his armpits and hauled him backwards into the house. His heels bounced down along the floor. His eyes, if they opened at all, rolled around the dark room. Often his clothing was soaked with beer sweat and vomit, so I stripped him in the shower and turned on the water. His hair matted down on his eyes. The pale skin stretched tight over the thin frame shivering under the cold.

"Come on," I said, and he lifted his chin to the stream for a moment before lowering it again. He was wrapped so deeply in his mind that he could not even feel the drops on his skin or hear my voice in his ear. Only his glistening ribs rising and falling against the skin confirmed that he was alive.

I've driven back from South Portland and parked outside Brian's apartment just to see what he will do. I take a few notes, sitting in the car, concerning Andrew's situation. When I speak to Gerald Dworkin, the chief coroner, I will tell him, without mentioning details, that Andrew is one of us. It is impossible to tell yet if he will develop the necessary discipline for the job. Those who find that discipline comes naturally do not make good coroners. Nor do those who find no self-discipline at all.

Brian leaves the house at nine, walks down State Street, and takes a left on Fore. I step out of the car and follow on foot, staying a block and a half behind. He throws a cigarette into the gutter and lights another. At the corner of Fore and Market he walks into Gritty's. I sit across the street on a bench. From here I can see him sit at the end of the bar, in the corner by himself. He has shaved, combed his hair, put on his best clothes—a golf shirt and blue jeans. The people there are his age, so they wouldn't know at first unless they looked closely at his dim, vacant eyes. He orders one drink after another, beginning with beer and moving to vodka. After an hour and a half a woman sits down next to him. He turns his head and I can see the jaw moving. He wipes his chin. After just five minutes the woman points across the room. She won't come back, and he probably knows that. Two hours pass. The woman has left with someone else. Most people have left. The young couples and groups of women in summer skirts have vanished, gone home. Groups of guys in football jerseys or muscle shirts tumble out of the bar and make their way back to their cars. The police cruiser passes by. I lower my head so they don't notice me. Four guys still in their softball uniforms pass by. One of them comes back to stand in front of me. His buddies don't notice at first.

"What gives you the right to sit on this bench all night?" the guy slurs. Slobber sprays onto my cheek. I sit back, cross my legs, and look up. "I seen you sitting here before." His friends have joined him by now. "I want to sit down." And he collapses next to me. For a moment I can see Brian again. The bar only has a few guys playing darts.

Another guy demands, "My friend wants to stretch out. Who do you think you are?"

I take out my coroner's badge and hold it up for him to see. He leans down and reads. When he looks from the badge to me I can see his eyes darting frantically over my face. He leans forward, grabs his friend by the shirt, and hauls him to his feet.

The bartender runs a finger across his throat when Brian asks for another beer. Brian doesn't react but he also doesn't let go of the mug. I'm up crossing the road. I have to wait for a car to pass. He stumbles across the room. He raises the glass over his head and hurls it against the dartboard. The five guys playing there circle him, and I jump out into the road without looking. A car screeches to a stop, the person leaning forward on the horn. I'm running now past the bouncer with my badge in my hand. He holds his hands up as if I might arrest him for not doing anything to stop the five guys pummeling Brian to the ground. Now they're kicking him in the stomach. I pull two guys back and grab one guy by the throat just as he is about to swing a stool into Brian's kidneys. The biggest of the guys grabs the badge out of my hand as I flash it forward.

"This is no cop's badge," he snorts and throws it back.

I roll Brian over. The blood pours out of his nose onto his old Dartmouth golf shirt.

"Get me some ice," I yell to the bartender, who hasn't changed his expression and is still wiping glasses. He looks at me but doesn't seem to hear.

"Get it yourself."

"Does it hurt?" I whisper.

Brian shakes his head slowly. Even the skin of his arm feels cold and lifeless as if the blood has already stopped flowing.

"Leave me alone," he says, closing his eyes.

"We have to get you to the hospital."

"There's no use. Just leave." He struggles to sit up, and refusing my help, manages to pull himself to his feet by the end of the bar. He sits down on one of the stools.

"We're closed, Brian," the bartender says. He's a friend of Brian's, but he never lifts a finger to help him. Brian doesn't want him to. The bartender doesn't even seem embarrassed or disturbed—he has a few more glasses to clean before he goes home. He sees my brother's type all the time.

"I'll leave when he's gone," Brian says, nodding his head toward me.

I wait outside for him to leave the bar, then follow him home to make sure he gets into the apartment.

It's just a few hours now from our morning shift, so I lie back in the car outside Brian's apartment and close my eyes. At seven in the morning he's headed down the street toward me. I roll down my window.

"Where are you headed today?" I ask.

"Don't know. Might head down to the noon AA meeting."

"Do you want me to pick you up there?"

"No. I'll have coffee with a bunch of the guys there afterwards."

Plans are being made to be somewhere else. He's tapping his foot against the curb, the toe coming out of the sneaker. The plans are in the foot. They're in the ash dangling like a crooked finger and then floating down to the pavement.

"Let me give you a ride. Anywhere you want to go."

"Let's just ride up to the Eastern Prom and back, to see the ocean."

He seems cheerful this morning—probably doesn't remember a thing from last night. He rolls the window down and flicks the ash out. At the prom the cool morning wind blows steady in from the south, rolls up the shore under our noses, and passes into the city. Brian walks down ahead of me with his arms outstretched—at first just slightly out to the side but extending up into the air as if reaching. His brown hair floats up, and it seems like he could fly. I think of Andrew's friend racing toward the ground without a chute. Brian thinks he will continue up over the giant elm at the edge of the park into the sky. The entire time I have been watching him fall, he has been waiting to rise.

Andrew arrives a minute ahead of schedule. He rests his coat on the back of the chair, places both hands on the desk, and stares ahead at the wall.

We head out to the car and turn on the scanner. We listen but do not respond. Not until they call specifically for us.

"Forty-five Thorton," the dispatcher says, but she is not speaking to us. An attempted suicide. Andrew reaches for the volume on the radio, but the announcement is over.

"We're only a mile from there," he says.

"They didn't call for us."

"We have to go."

I shake my head.

"I have to go!" he shouts this time, grabs for the door handle, and pushes it open at forty-eight miles an hour. I pull off the road.

"Shut that door!" I yell. He pulls the door closed but doesn't take his hand off the handle. "You are not in love with that woman. You think you are, but you're not." He sets his jaw and grips the door handle until the veins emerge on his forearm. I realize he will go there on foot if he has to. I may as well drive him.

An ambulance and two cruisers are parked outside with their lights spinning in the rain. The four officers stand out front in slickers talking to each other. The first neighbor we spoke to comes to her window, still holding her cat, and slides the curtain to the side. She pushes her glasses further up along her wrinkled bumpy nose and squints at us. The dry lips part around her yellowed teeth. The other neighbor paces back and forth in front of her house carrying one screaming kid in each arm. All three are soaked. The kids cling to their mother's neck with both hands.

"I was going to stop by," the woman calls to us frantically. "I know you told me I should stop by."

"Go back inside," I say to her.

"My kids wouldn't settle down. I was going to stop by when they took a nap." The rain has soaked through her bleached hair and run across her cracked lower lip. Andrew runs ahead to the porch, where the medics have just emerged with their equipment. I catch Andrew by the shoulder before he makes it to the steps. I stand behind him, wrap my arms around his body, and press him to me as I would the next of kin.

"I want you to look at your watch. Take out your notebook," I whisper into his ear.

He looks up to one of the medics, who replaces tubes and wires in a large metal case, closes, then locks the lid. The man rests against the side of the house and lets out a long breath.

"He's giving up," Andrew says. "He's giving up too soon."

"He did all he could do."

The other medic, kneeling down over his equipment, gives me a nod. The motor on their ambulance is still running. They have another call—I can hear the radio from their cab. They have to move on. They both start walking toward the back of the ambulance, where they store the gear. They don't smile or cry but just go about their business.

"Don't go in there unless you understand what we have to do. All right?" I ask. He shakes his head, the hair on the back of his neck brushing against my nose. "The guys from the morgue are going to come," I whisper. "We'll ride in the van with them." I can feel his shoulder blades pinching against my chest.

Inside he lays his hand on her cheek and buries his face in his arm. I rest my hand on his back where the muscles erupt as if sustaining punches from inside. Abandoned by breath and voice and heat—things so invisible we can't believe they ever existed—the body has become a shell of cold skin and eyes, the outline of the person. When this melts away it seems as if the person never existed at all. It's hard for him to see how it could be important to protect her now when he could not protect her before. But he should know by now that we are not like everyone else. We protect the dead so that others can believe in life.

Hydrophobia

Last Tuesday, after Roger's barbecue and an official demonstration of his new gas-powered Weber involving salmon petrified into coal and a meal of chips and salsa, I woke up at two in the morning kicking my legs in bed like a man trying to win at the five-hundred-meter backstroke. I jumped up and down next to the bed for a few minutes, but still they twitched, so I ran up and down the stairs half a dozen times in my socks and boxer shorts. Laura came out of the study, holding her reading glasses, and Sara opened her door to ask if there were robbers or a fire, her two worst nighttime fears.

"It's all right," I said. "Daddy's just having a problem with his legs."

I fell right to sleep after tucking Sara back into bed and kissing her on the forehead. The next morning I woke up and drove to the base to fly our regular training mission over Trescott, Molunkus, Howland, and Deblois, and further north toward

Canada, where you can see nothing but acres of pine forest; I thought the problem was over, but that night I woke up with my legs kicking again. I had to walk outside for twenty minutes before the irritation would stop. Laura looked up from her books and suggested I see a doctor about it. I don't know what she meant by this—I am a doctor. Then last night I practically jumped out of bed like a sprinter and ended up walking even further down the road in my bathrobe and sneakers.

Finally I decided to consult Roger, the guy who rented us our house here, now a golfing friend of mine and also a neurologist. I told him I could stop the kicking if I concentrated hard enough, but then a wave of energy seemed to travel up over my stomach and chest heading for my head, which sent me into a panic. I also mentioned climbing the stairs and taking walks as a way of solving the problem temporarily. He eyed the fairway, wiggled his butt, sucked the snot out of his nose, which runs constantly because of a deviated septum he refuses to fix, and finally looked down at the ball. A roll of fat slung over the lip of his turtleneck, making him look much older than thirty-eight. The club cocked back, paused, and swayed through in a neat circle, and the ball, shrinking in size as it sped down the alley of green oaks, arched up and over the sand pits.

"Try drinking over it," he said without moving from the finished position.

He had me sit on the edge of the golf cart while he tapped my kneecaps with the handle of his club, and when that seemed normal he waved me down and twisted his hand. I turned and he pulled my shirt up in back, digging his index finger into spots along the side of my spine. "Hmmm," he said.

"What?"

"I think I hear meowing."

"You hear what?"

"You'd better come in for a CAT scan, but not until I beat you to death on the next six holes."

We played the last six holes, and he kept making cracks that I was seeing my last game ever, I'd better make it a good one.

Laura doesn't notice I have come into her study this morning until I lean over her head and look down at the screen. She finds my hand on her shoulder and squeezes the palm as she rereads the last sentence just added to her dissertation:

> Cassiodorus realized his plans through the establishment at Squillace of a monastery, which he called Vivarium, from the fish ponds (vivaria) on its grounds. Here he spent the remainder of his long life with his monks, guiding them in their work.

"Did you meet with Roger?" she asks without turning around.

"Yep."

"What does he think you should do?"

"Have a CAT scan."

"Does he really, or is he just kidding around?"

"I can't tell this time."

Laura reaches forward to type the first word of the next sentence: *Cassiodorus.* Even after two years of living here, her books and the good dishes from her grandmother, even her nice shoes and the camel hair coat I bought for her, still sit in boxes on the floor next to the desk. She lived out of boxes when I met her in Cambridge and she was renting a walk-up in Somerville. At first, after we were married and the air force provided for us enough so she could quit her job, she seemed interested in pursuing law—her father, it turned out, had been a convict. I asked her further questions about him and her childhood, but she would say no more, and never has, about any of it. After she told me and after we had made love and were lying naked on top of the stripped bed letting the fans cool us off in the middle of a swampy Cambridge heat wave, she said, "Now I can trust you completely," but I sensed she was guessing at what I wanted to hear. I had worked hard through the academy and in flight school and in my first year in med school, alone and free to do whatever I wanted, I didn't care what she said as long as she kept talking in a voice that seemed as lilting and soft as satin. It could be that on one of these nights I had led her to believe that I would become the kind of doctor you saw around who lived in Belmont or Lexington, driving in to Mass General while his family stayed at home and the kids attended Concord Academy or Buckingham Brown and Nichols. I did not tell her until after we were married how much I love the feeling of rising into the sky and even the rules and uniforms, how simple the air force makes life. I remember one night she said she would not want to have kids unless she could send them away to one of these schools, and I said nothing.

Shortly after we were married she gave up her interest in law, saying it seemed banal, and she started talking nonstop about Italy—Florence in Dante's time, Bologna, a city still untouched by tourism. She talked through the summer nights in Cambridge, and I closed my eyes, loving the sound of places—the Uffizi, the Medici Chapel—that I never really cared to see. In her mouth they were musical and physical, like a drug. We were planning a trip to Italy until it became clear that Sara's arrival would absorb all our money, and then she lost interest in Italy and wanted to study the theory of history. Now she tells me her doctorate is almost done, but she won't tell me what the title is or anything specific about the subject. When I ask her what period or place she is writing about, she tells me that kind of history is over.

Through the window I see Sara back in the woods near the poison ivy, her school dress covered with dirt marks and her hand in the air clutching a model F-14. She makes shooting sounds with her lips and explosions that come up from her throat as I approach. I made the mistake of telling her one day when we were discussing what she wants to be when she grows up that I would never let her be a carrier pilot, so now that's all she talks about before bed, aside from robbers, the house burning down, and the possibility of the world ending. She takes my hand and we wander out of the pines, the F-14 dangling with its nose down and Sara yanking on my arm.

In addition to my job as doctor on the base I have, for some time now, been flying bombers, descending out of the night sky to the neat rows of bright lights marking the runway. The plane floats down, like a giant egg I always imagine, under the gentle pressure of my palm against the lever. I'm not so young anymore that people would say "Struck down in his prime," although they might say "Too bad." As a married doctor without gray hair sent here for a stint at the air base to poke people and occasionally fly, I'm automatically suspected of just wanting to do my time and get out.

Really, unless patients start dying, the reputation of a basic mechanics doctor like me depends on what one does in public on the base and how one touches people in the infirmary. I've learned that most of the guys don't like to be touched at all; they want to know all the reasons why before you do it, though some guys are secretly like cats and love to be touched delicately at the ends of their shoulders and just above the hip. I have come to like living in this town, and in this cottage on the ocean, knowing Jerry down at Boynton's and Francine who cuts hair, but Laura has made me promise we will move to the city when I am done with the air force. "When the air force is done with me," I always correct her, though she no longer smiles at this.

I sit on the wraparound porch looking down at the cove and beyond that at the bay and the lighthouse on Southport Island while Sara puts the finishing touches on her fairy house. The sound of Laura's fingers tapping on the keyboard upstairs reminds me of mice pattering in the attic above my bedroom when I was a kid. Sara stands back to check her work, bending her head sideways.

"Can we watch the fairies move into the house?" she asks. I tell her no, they will only move in when we aren't watching.

"How tall are the fairies?"

"They come in different sizes," I say. She kneels down and peers in through the doorway of the stick-and-bark wall that quivers precariously in the breeze.

"We'd better make it taller in case the fairies are tall," she says and runs off the porch into the woods for more sticks. Watching her run, just lifting her bare feet over fallen oaks, I'm afraid she will trip and fall. When she stops running, I rise to my feet and creak over the pine boards to the study, someone's old bedroom, where Laura has set up her computer. She wants to finish by the end of the month, so she can send it to her committee.

When we met at the bar where she worked, she was studying at the local community college. That first night she smelled so much of lavender and rose it was hard to believe she was made of the same flesh as the bodies lying dead on the metal tables waiting for our scalpels. I had spent years in bunks, rising to horns and whistles, living among other men and boys, eating off metal trays. Her shoulder and arm were as hard as ripe pears. I feel the same disbelief now, resting my hand on her back, that I did then. Out the window I can see Sara examining a spot on the ground, kneeling there, as if in prayer, and rubbing her hands in the pine needles. Laura doesn't look up or stop typing as I lean over.

"I guess I'll go over to County and meet with Roger," I say. She nods her head.

"Daddy!" Sara calls from outside. She has already forgotten about the fairy house and is now running off down the trail toward the cove. I follow the crooked, uneven path spotted with moss and slippery, lichen-covered rocks. Sara waits for me, standing in her bathing suit with her back to the water, her shorts and T-shirt lying in a crumpled pile on the sand. When I sit down on a log, she turns and walks away from me into the water up to her knees, then her waist. The tiny waves lift her up to her tiptoes and back down again. She turns to look at me—she has been afraid of swimming the last few summers after a time in early spring when she fell off the dock at Roger's house when we weren't looking, and she was wearing a thick wool coat. I turned to see her head rise above the water, her eyes watching me, before she vanished beneath the surface. I jumped in after her, and everyone was fine—she swallowed a little water but didn't even catch a cold in the end. I blamed myself for months, but it's true, what Roger said, that you can't have your eye on them for every second of their lives. Laura and I have tried to coax her to follow us in these last few summers, but she never would. This, suddenly, is the farthest I have seen her go.

"Aren't you cold?" I ask.

She shakes her head, though I can see she is starting to shiver. She reaches her arm down, stretches with her chin raised, and finally bends her whole body until she vanishes completely. Her head pops up with the water soaking through her hair down into her mouth, and in her hand she clutches a large blue mussel.

"What do you have there?" I ask, but she won't answer. She is busy trying to open the two halves, which have clammed shut. First her shoulders, then her arms and her whole body shake. I yell for her to come out of the water before she catches cold. She looks at me for a moment before trudging through the water and plopping down on the sun-bleached log amidst the sea grass—too late in the cycle now for mosquitoes and too early in the season for green flies. I lay a towel over her shoulders, but she pushes it off and shakes more violently as the cove in front of us darkens and a gust of wind washes away the salty warmth that has been collecting around us. Sensing someone behind us, I turn around but see only the weathered gray shingles of the house face, the second floor hanging over the porch like the upper jaw of a gaping, toothless mouth, the windows watery and dark and the thick, green pines swaying above. Sara lays the mussel down on a flat rock, picks up a heavy stick next to my foot, and drops it on top of the blue shell. With her fingers she scrapes the gooey contents out and lays them on my knee.

Laura is coming down the path. I can hear the twigs snapping and the wet moss squishing beneath her heels.

"Look at this, Mom," Sara says.

Laura walks right by us down to the water's edge, removes her robe onto a dry rock, and adjusts the strap of her green bathing suit as she wades slowly into the water. Sara follows, lifting her feet carefully in and out and remaining four or five feet to the right of her mother—this time she won't go deeper than her ankles. Laura dives forward, her long swimmer's body arching and vanishing down with a light slurp, not even a splash, and Sara scans over the water waiting for her to come up. She finally does, nearly a minute later, on the other side of the cove.

Sara rides with me out to the county hospital, playing with the radio in our plain white government-issue sedan.

"What are they going to do?"

"Just take a look at my brain," I say.

"I can do that," she declares, rising up to her knees and leaning on my shoulder to see inside my ear. "All I see are hairs in there. You have a hairy brain."

"Did you bring your coloring book?" She nods her head dramatically up and down, still looking in my ear.

"I wish Mommy was dead," she says flatly.

"Sara," I say in my serious voice. "Don't say that."

"I do," she says.

"She is busy now. She's trying to finish her work. It won't always be this way. Understand?" She nods her head just a little and sits back down in her seat.

At the hospital, Roger holds her hand as I lie down on what he calls the sled.

"What's going to happen?" Sara whines. I wanted to leave her with Roger's wife, Nancy, a nurse on the floor, but he insisted Sara should see it's no big deal.

"We're just going to slide him in there and look for cats," Roger says, lifting Sara up so she can see into the giant cylinder with an opening wide and tall enough for a body.

"What's in there? There are cats in there? Noooo."

"Lots of cats holding little cameras that can see into your brain." Roger holds her sideways and tickles her under the chin until she giggles wildly.

The hydraulic motor, like the motors controlling the wing flaps or the bay doors of my plane, moves the sled into the cylinder. Sara walks next to my head until I vanish, and I hear her yell, "No, don't go."

"Don't worry, sweetheart," Roger says, nudging her slightly, causing her rubber heels to squeak against the polished floors. The noise echoes off the bare white walls. "We play music for him in there. He'll be fine." And then I am inside, like a bullet in a chamber, with my eyes closed listening to the hum like the steady drone of a plane's jet engine. Not so many years ago, before Sara's birth, before I met Laura, I flew hundreds of miles through darkness, and when the navigator gave the word to the bombardier, the hydraulic doors opened and the plane leapt up slightly from the sudden absence of weight. We continued on in a slow curve and heard nothing, saw nothing of the burning desert we had left behind and thousands of feet below. That was before I was trained as a resident to treat burn and shrapnel wounds and saw the flesh broken apart or melted and heard the person screaming in the emergency room, teeth bared and eyes clamped shut.

At home I lie on the couch downstairs for a nap as Sara climbs the steps to Laura's study. I hear her feet enter the room, stand behind her mother, and turn back around—the typing continues without pause. In this house you can hear every noise because only the outside walls are insulated.

I don't wake until late in the afternoon, when I open my eyes to the sound of the phone ringing.

"I'm looking at your brain," Roger says, and I can hear the negative rattling in the background as he holds it up to the light. As I wait for him to go on, I can also hear the shower running upstairs.

"Well?"

"The part that keeps bad ideas from escaping seems a little damaged, but the rest looks normal to me."

"Normal."

"And you owe me fifty dollars from yesterday's game. If you had a tumor I was going to forget about it, but not now."

At first I think it might be raining and not the shower running as I climb the stairs, but the faucets squeak shut and Laura steps in front of the mirror. I can hear the drops of water falling off her body and splatting on the plastic mat. The fog has rolled across the bay and sifted through the pines. Walking down the hall, I find Laura drying herself. The windows also drip with moisture from her shower. The fog outside is so thick that little drops will form on my sweater if I sit still, even in the living room. If I go outside, the drops will bead across the top of my hair. Water collects in a pool around her feet on the bare wooden floor. She lays one hand on her left butt cheek, as people do when they think no one is looking, and looks out the window facing the woods. Settling the robe over her shoulders and pulling it tight around the middle, she walks straight up to the window and rests her palms against the panes of warped glass. Outside patches of fog an arm's width mingle with the branches and slide around trunks. An old chair next to her leg is losing its stuffing in the arms where someone's elbows rested, and the paint has worn off the floor where heels scraped.

Laura returns to her desk and leans over the computer again, reaching down with an index finger extended to backspace, maybe, or to add a missing comma. The finger stops short, however, and she looks back out the window. I try to imagine what she is thinking, her mind floating somewhere in the chivalry, armor, and disease of the years 300 to 1500. I know her focus is narrower, but she has not told me which years or even which countries—France, I assume, but maybe England. I know of the Henrys and William the Conqueror. She sits down in the chair next to the desk and tears pour out of her eyes. When she sees me, she quickly wipes her face clean.

"What's wrong?" I ask, kneeling down in front of her. She shakes her head and wraps her arms around her stomach. I lay my hand on her arm, but she flinches away; her whole body tenses and she closes her eyes. When she opens them again, she bursts out crying even harder. I sit back against the bed and wait for her to stop. She does, in moments, but then stands and walks down the hall, and I sit in the old chair, placing my shoes on the ruts in the floor. The old floorboards creak as she descends the stairs. Behind the curtain covering the closet sit the shoes of whoever Roger bought this house from in three neat, polished pairs: work boots, thirty-year-old dress shoes saved for occasions that never arrived, and sneakers.

Hours before dawn, Sara sound asleep, my legs act up again. I put on my coat, tiptoe down the stairs into the shadowy dark, and creep through the woods trying to tire myself out enough to sleep, and I wonder who might be watching me from the trees. Smaller pines hiding in the shadows behind the trunks of large oaks look like people creeping along parallel to the trail. Without warning, my legs start to run down toward Route 32, where I pick up the white line and start sprinting into darkness. There are no streetlights or houses for miles, and my legs move faster—it feels as though I might be moving thirty miles an hour or more, though I know that's impossible, and my lungs open up wider to swallow more air. I move to the faint center double yellow line and speed up even more, swinging my arms long and wide. Around the corner a mile or so from the house a truck with its high beams glaring barrels down the road toward me. I'm running so fast, downhill now, that I can't stop or slow. The truck pulls off to the side of the road and lets me pass. At the bottom of the hill I stumble on a pothole and fly through the air until my hands grind against the asphalt and I roll over and over.

The truck has turned around and pulled up beside me, and I recognize the guy now as Frank, the carpenter who looks after Roger's many properties around the area. He rolls the window down and sticks his narrow, unshaven face out into the damp air.

"I thought that was you, Dr. McKenna. You all right? You want a ride back up to the house?"

I stand without responding and climb in the cab.

"I was out for a little walk," I start to explain, looking down at the tear in my jeans. "And I just started to run." Frank nods but doesn't say anything until we pull up to the edge of the driveway.

"Better stay out of the middle of the road," he says and gives me the same toothy smile he uses to tell you the part for the shower will take two weeks to arrive.

I walk down beside the house to the cove. The water is nearly flat, the waves lazy, hanging in the air before coming down, and the air is warm and calm. I stand at the edge, stepping back as the water laps up to my shoes, and I can see the stars reflected in the surface of the water. They would help me navigate the world if I were the kind of pilot who traveled the seas hundreds of years ago and not someone who eyes a lighted instrument panel, reaching out for buttons and levers, crossing hundreds of miles in a matter of minutes.

I hear feet crunching on dried seaweed behind me, and when I turn there is Sara's moonlit face and her nightgown flowing around thin legs. I sit down next to her against a piece of driftwood. She sits at first but then suddenly stands up again and races down to the water. She plays this game often: chasing the ebb out toward the sea and running back from the flow. She giggles and her hair flies up into the moonlight as her feet churn away from the water.

"Come here," I hear myself say in a gruff voice, though I only mean to protect her. She stops running, rests her hands on her hips. My face is lit by the moon while hers stays hidden in the shadow.

"No," she states and rushes down the beach, stops, turns, and rushes back again. In the dark her feet don't even seem to touch the sand. With no warning she veers away from the wash and keeps running toward me instead of turning back to chase the flow, stopping so suddenly and so close that sand lifts up and spreads over the front of my jeans. She leans forward and places one hand on each one of my cheeks. I pull her close and whisper that I love her.

Laura has come down the trail and stands next to us. I can see the backs of her blue-jean legs as she walks forward down the beach to the water. After watching her mother walk up to her waist, Sara grabs hold of my index finger and leans back like a dock worker hauling on a line. Her heels dig into the sand and she tenses her face. I stand up and follow her down to the water's edge.

Laura leans down and dives into the water. It is as though she ceases to exist until her white face appears in the moonlight moving forward along the surface of the water, a disembodied ghost. "Come in," she says. "The water's warm tonight." As I walk forward I realize it's true. The water is warm tonight like layers of soft down and silk seeping between my pants and skin. I lean down into the water and stand back up, and Laura swims in front of me. Her face under my palm burns with fever or tears, and it seems that the whole ocean warms with her.

"Come here, sweetheart," Laura says, not to me, and I turn to see Sara standing at the water's edge looking out at us. She takes one step into the water but stops and looks down. At night you can't see the bottom and your feet seem to vanish forever at the waterline. "Come on," Laura says in a sob. Sara turns and for a moment I think she will just walk away from us back up to the house. Laura's hands start to drop, but then I see that Sara has just backed up for a running start. When her feet hit the water, spray flies up in a fan until she falls forward, headfirst, and vanishes underwater. The surface is empty except for the ripples illuminated by the moon. Laura stays bent over with her hands out and waits, too long, it seems, but in moments Sara rises up into her arms, and in the luminescent light I can see Sara's bright teeth and hear a trill of giggles as they spin around together in a circle. Sara's feet fan out and she clings to her mother's arms. I know the ocean is cold enough to kill in minutes and empty except for the kind of hard silver creatures hurling through the darkness with no direction and no memory. Not tonight, not for us, I tell myself, as I lean into the water and float on my back looking up at the patterns, angels and warriors, millions of light-years away. Tonight the water is warmer than my skin, and Sara whirls through the air filling our ears with laughter. It is hard to believe, listening to the sound of such joy, that we will not live forever.

Halloween

She was having the best game of her life the day our father fell from the sky. The tennis balls were rocketing, starting low, rising just over the net, and dropping in the far corner. Her coach was hungry, his stomach growling, his arms and legs like rubber bands, and he was bored. The sky over the training fields had turned orange and violet. The tanks, half a mile east, killed their engines for the day. Troops marched in formation right by the courts on their way to the mess hall. She followed the ball with complete attention as if her life depended on the perfection of its path.

I am her brother, two years older. Back then I was much more interested in the meandering path of a daydream than in the perfection of a single act like a swing. The beaches a mile from the base looked out over uninterrupted ocean, and the temperature in October reminded me of summer in Maine, where we had lived until just a year earlier. A friend named Andy, a short kid whose father, like mine, was a pilot serving in a war thousands of miles away, lay spread-eagled in the sand with a long stick wedged in his armpit. He was playing dead, waiting for his mom to take us home. I was picking up sticks and half shells off the beach and throwing them back into the ocean, dreaming, as always, of the places I would arrive, and the person I would become far in the future, though I had no idea how to get there. Olive-green Phantoms roared overhead, three in formation, streaking over the land and finally darting off into the sky. One day, I thought, I would sit in the cockpit, made anonymous by the oxygen mask, helmet, and dark glasses, serving some higher purpose. But when I looked back out over the ocean, I pictured myself there, in a small boat. In dreams, as in life, I have never traveled but always arrived. And I had never once considered that the world I dreamed was not the world in which I lived. I picked up a piece of driftwood off the beach and rushed at my friend Andy, to stab him once more, the pretend enemy, to make sure he was dead and my child's world, then and now, safe from a life I have never been able to imagine.

Andy's mom arrived and stood on the dunes, arms akimbo with the sun behind her, a dark cut-out shape of a woman.

There was nothing more silent at Cherry Point than the marines eating dinner. The machines, gunshots, clicking heels, and shouted commands all ceased very suddenly and always at the same time, even as the days grew shorter into winter. When the silence hit, my sister, Heidi, stood up straight and let the tennis ball bounce by. The tennis coach walked forward hoping to end the lesson early, but she quickly hit another ball in his direction, which he smoothly returned, backing up for the full swing so as not to look bad. Nobody liked the tennis coach. He was always having some problem.

The empty pangs of the ball against the strings and the muffled screech of tennis shoes against hardtop were the only sounds. Eleven other courts stood empty, the players gone home for dinner.

Finally the coach let one of the balls go by and stepped up toward the net. "Enough for today," he said. She stayed in a crouch, racket cocked back as if he were a ball coming over the net. He stopped and tapped the net with his racket, turned around, and started to pick up stray balls. She leaned against the fence. All the balls were on his side of the net. She could play all night without eating or sleeping, driving herself straight into her future, which she could see always just on the horizon. The coach walked around the net waving his racket to get her attention. "Ready?" he said and headed out the gate.

She followed, leaving her racket against the fence on the court as if she were coming right back.

"Your mom's late," the coach said in the parking lot.

She wanted to say something but she couldn't. She was trying to remember something. She had forgotten.

"You told her six, right?" the coach asked while combing the parking lot and the officers' lot below.

She focused on the back of his head. "Yes," she said. "You can leave. She'll be here in a minute."

"No, I can't do that," he said. "But I do have to be somewhere. I bet you do too. What are you going to be?"

"A cat."

"A cat?"

"Yes."

"Do you have a costume?"

"Yes, but it's in the car."

"Your mom's car?"

She nodded. "You can leave," she said, and then remembered

her tennis racket and told him she would be right back. She watched her shoes moving like two little white-shelled turtles along the blacktop. The racket was still there and one of the stray balls.

When she returned to the parking lot the coach was gone. You couldn't even hear his car anymore he had driven away so fast. No other cars came down the road, so she went back to the court and hit the ball over the net. She switched sides and hit it again. She delighted in the idea of how much faster the ball would travel when she turned thirteen. Then she would practice into the night, improving the accuracy of her shot. The ball would land exactly where she pictured it would. Thirteen seemed like the year.

It would be dark soon, because the first soldiers were coming out of the mess hall, smoking and pushing each other lightly. She stood in the empty parking lot with the tennis racket and watched them pass by. Back then you could buy beer out of a machine on the base, so that's where they were going, to sit around and drink. Heidi watched them while walking down the parking lot. Then she tripped.

One of the soldiers broke off from the others, walked up to her, and held out his hand, in which an unlit cigarette lay wedged between two fingers. "Are you okay?" he asked.

"Come on," another soldier said.

"Yes, I'm fine," Heidi said, picking herself up.

The soldier turned around to frown at his friends, who were waving for him to hurry up.

"Are you sure?" he said. "I'm a medic, you know. It's my job to fix people."

"My mother's coming to pick me up," she said.

"Where is she?" the soldier asked.

"She's coming to get me."

"I hope soon," he said. "It's getting dark, you know?"

"Yes," she said. "I know."

"You know," he said, "I have a little girl just like you, only she lives far away."

"Does she play tennis?" Heidi asked.

"Well," he said, "I don't think she does. Maybe a little. Her name's Wendy."

Heidi nodded and looked up at the soldier with the unlit cigarette, and just as she expected, he was looking somewhere else. "Goodbye," he said, turning around. "Don't stay out in the dark."

"No," she said.

The tanks at dusk looked a little like elephants resting with their trunks straight out. Held at attention that way. Half resting, half scared. Heidi walked to the edge of the parking lot and turned right down Route 77, which led to our house, five miles away. A cat trotted toward her along the road. It had emerged from the motor pool, and as it approached, Heidi bent down on one knee, holding her hands out. But the big orange tom cat with the narrowed eyes and seeming grin trotted right by. A determined cat. She turned to watch him go and saw a small band of monsters, ghouls, and spirits who lived in houses on the base. All boys about her age carrying shopping bags to be filled with candy. They ran toward her screaming and gurgling, their arms waving in the air. They stopped in front of her, dropped their arms, and silently stared at her. She would know each one of them from school, if she could see under their masks.

"Aren't you scared of us?" Dracula asked.

"Why should I be?" she said. "You're David's brother."

"How did you know?" he demanded, stepping back.

"Your voice," she said.

A boy-soldier dressed in oversized fatigues, a helmet, and a gas mask said, "What are you supposed to be?" From inside the mask his voice sounded smothered by distance, as if he was yelling from a hundred yards away.

"I'm not anything," she said.

"You're Heidi," another one of them said. He looked like a wolf or a bear.

"Yes," she said, "I am."

All four stood staring at her. Then a woman further down the road called, "Boys!" and they all fled toward her. She must have been one of their mothers. She would lead them down to the other side of 77, where most of the houses sat. Heidi watched them until they were tiny stumps that blended together and suddenly bolted off the road to knock on someone's door. The road was empty again.

Then another speck appeared and moved toward her. After a few moments, she could see that it was an army jeep, driven by the soldier she had recently been talking to.

"We've been looking for you," he said after pulling to a stop. "We didn't think you should walk home by yourself." A couple of the others were sitting in the backseat; one of them had just tumbled there from the front. "Climb in. We'll give you an escort."

She picked up her tennis racket and walked around in front of the jeep, threw the racket in first, and then pulled herself up.

"Where to?" the soldier asked.

"I want to go home," she said.

"I know that," he said, smiling at her. "Where's that?"

"Down the road." She pointed.

"You'll tell me when we're getting close?"

"Yes," she answered.

In a few minutes she would be there, walk down the concrete

path, up the steps, turn the knob, and the smell of baked chicken would draw her in. This is how it usually happened. I was already at home sitting on the couch, waiting for her. As always I felt like I was living in her future. Not far enough to warn her, just far enough to know.

A car approached the jeep from a distance. You could see forever, because there were no hills or dips in the road. As it grew larger she could see the Chevrolet grille and the distinctive squarehead lights of her mother's station wagon. Standing up in the jeep, she started waving frantically at the station wagon long before its driver could have seen her.

"Sit down," the soldier said, but she kept it up, yelling her mother's name into the forty-mile-an-hour wind.

"Please, sit down!" the soldier yelled, and this time grabbed her by the waist with one hand and yanked her down hard against the seat. She banged her arm on top of the windshield as she sat down. "You'll get hurt," he said as she held her arm.

The station wagon slowed and pulled off the road. So did the soldier. "It's all right," he said. "She's seen you."

Before the jeep even stopped she had jumped out, hit the ground scraping her knee, and started running for her mother. Halfway there, tears blurred the familiar shape of the woman stepping out of the driver's seat. Heidi tripped in front of the car and a woman's long-nailed, delicately thin, but horribly dry hands pulled her up by the waist and let her stand, wobbling. Heidi wiped her eyes clean, embarrassed now, wondering what had just happened since it happened so fast, and looked up to find my friend Andy's mother. Andy still sat quietly in the backseat, looking at his feet in the shadows like a criminal. I had said goodbye to him only a few minutes before. His mother, Mrs. Stevenson, put her hand behind Heidi's head and stroked her hair. "Did you hurt yourself?" she asked, stepping back as if afraid of the little girl. Then, without waiting for an answer, she gently pushed Heidi forward by the back of the head toward the passenger seat, opened the door, and waited for her to climb in. Mrs. Stevenson went around the other side and sat behind the wheel. The car was still running.

The soldier, standing in front of the jeep, looked at Heidi and at the woman he took for her mother. Heidi knew he was looking, but she would not lift her head up as the car turned around. She resented everyone's kindness. The soldier remained standing in the road, still waiting or uncertain.

Neither Andy nor his mother spoke during the short trip down the road. Mrs. Stevenson reached out once, keeping her eyes glued to the yellow line, and moved her hand up and down along the back of Heidi's head. At that time of the evening, the woods, which line both sides of the road, were darker than peering down into the open ocean. The tall grass lining the asphalt was the color of old, yellowed leather, and the sky above the trees was on fire. The moon was above the fire, sitting in the faded blue. I could see it all from the bay window in our living room, and I could imagine how Heidi saw it, running before her eyes like a tired commercial. I wanted to meet her on the front lawn. I had seen Mrs. Stevenson leave and knew about how long the trip would take. Much shorter than I thought, it turned out. But I could not move from the couch. I was paralyzed by the slightest idea.

As Mrs. Stevenson pulled into the driveway, Heidi couldn't look up to see her house because of the guilt she felt for the soldier. She could imagine how he would have looked if she had glanced up as they drove away. She imagined him standing there in the road watching the back of the station wagon vanish, and as the station wagon pulled to a stop, she wanted to turn back to the base and find him. To thank him. But the car's engine had been turned off, and there was something final about that. Then she remembered her tennis racket still sitting in the jeep, traveling back to the motor pool to sit there or in the soldier's room.

Mrs. Stevenson went around to the passenger side of the car, opened the door, and held out her hand. That morning Heidi and I had made preparations for Halloween. We had tied a bunched-up towel to the top of a broomstick, covered it in a white sheet, and stuck it in the ground. We had tied a string around the towel for the neck and colored in eyes and a mouth. Next to that we had covered two or three milk crates with a sheet and a carved-out pumpkin. At the feet of these creatures sat three smaller uncarved pumpkins that we would later use for a pie.

I heard the car door slam and could see Heidi moving toward the front steps. Mrs. Stevenson hung on to the passenger door as if she were about to fall down. Heidi stopped when she saw that our ghosts had been ripped from the ground and piled at the head of the driveway near the trash. The carved-out pumpkin lay next to the ghosts. Two other men in green suits, not the men from the jeep, sat in an olive-green military sedan, having yet to drive away after talking to our mother. Everyone on the air base knew about these men, who occasionally came to visit the wives of pilots.

"David!" Heidi screamed my name, angry and afraid. "David!"

I stood up in the living room, buried there, it seemed, and the front door was just opening. I started for the doorway, am still rushing there years later, though our mother always arrives first, looming above the front steps. If I could alter that moment when Heidi looked up at her drained, white face, blue eyeliner running down both cheeks, then I still believe we could have the lives we dreamed of on those long beaches, our hands, half the size they are now, sifting through the sand for shells. My mother's two white hands stood in the air, reaching out, and strands of hair stuck to her chin that moved up and down as if she were speaking. But no one was speaking for miles around. There was nothing that could be said.

Afterlife

My brother Roy stood naked in the falling snow reading an article about the temperature of the ocean in Florida. It also described oleander, jasmine, rose of Sharon around the knees. And in the mouth: flowering peach, coconut, mango, the shock of a lemon plucked and squeezed onto the tongue—all from a *Travel and Leisure* they gave him at Mercy Hospital. Down there, it said, you could play tennis in white shorts while the palms waved like gills. He came inside from the deck, shut the door, climbed under the covers of his bed, and started to read aloud. I could see a photo of a long blond woman in a pink bikini reclined against a palm tree in front of white sand and clear blue water. Roy's breath rose up from a passageway he had made around his mouth with the wool blankets. The kerosene heater had gone out, and the afternoon light streamed in through the window, turning the empty walnut bookcases of what had been someone's library a soft, warm brown.

Roy had never been to Florida, but he was sure people there must be happy with the condition of their skin. No matter how much aloe he applied, he scratched his arms and the side of his face and picked flakes of skin out from under his fingernails to show me. "See this," he said, reaching his hand up toward my face. I turned my head away. "I'm getting out of the state. Eight o'clock tonight, on that bus." He had decided just the day before in the hospital when I visited to head south.

I suggested we wait until spring. That's all we had talked about for the last few months while going to AA meetings and trying to find work. "Just wait for spring," people in AA had said, and even though it was a trick to keep us from running once again, I believed them. "Trust in God," they said, and it seemed that God would wait for the sun, for the ice to melt. He might even wait until Roy and I made it out into the salt waves in August, until the sand burned our feet. It was worth holding on just a few more months to see.

"Why wait when you can go down to it?" Roy wanted to know. He set the magazine down on the blankets. "You can pick fish out of the waves and toss them into your mouth," he said with his eyes closed and his hands calmly folded.

All we had to do was wait, I felt sure of it, for once in our lives. After all, two days of piercing blue skies had just passed. The icicles outside our window had started to melt, a drip a minute, and it seemed possible that something other than snow might fall from the sky.

Roy stood up out of bed again and walked to the picture window and the door that opened onto the roof of a garage. He opened the door and held his hand out to where a few tiny flakes landed in his palm. It was so cold outside, so cold in the room, maybe even the skin of his palm had fallen in temperature so quickly that the snow didn't melt but slowly accumulated on his hand like a pile of salt. He closed the door. The wind whistled between the cracks in the frames, two quick bursts. Despite the wedges, tape, and caulking, the windows rattled, and I wondered about the pneumonia that had put him in the hospital. He stood in the middle of the room facing down the length of the apartment, formerly a Victorian townhouse, now an old firetrap rented under the table, and rested his hands on his hips.

"I can't find my ass," he said and left his jaw hanging. "They took my ass in the hospital." He had walked out before discharge, sometime between bath and dinner, taking the robe with him and the potted plant from the waiting area.

"Maybe they took it down the hall for testing," I suggested.

"An ass scan."

He was twenty pounds lighter, and his head had narrowed to the shape of an ax blade. In the bathroom next door I wrapped myself tighter in the old down jacket held together with duct tape as he lowered himself into the tub. Roy had started out like me, as the people in AA had told us: morning and night on his knees, but now his idea of prayer was to sit in the bath and cup the water from the tap over his head. Steam rose from the tight, black curls and from the tops of his closed lids down over his rough skin.

The door downstairs clanged open, and the footsteps of Andy's boyfriend climbed in a steady, even, drunken ascent. Bo reached the top step and entered the kitchen, where Andy was baking cookies for Roy's send-off. We could hear Andy's muffled gulps for air meant to inform Bo of his disgust, but Bo was probably already passed out and didn't care. He creaked his long body over the rusty springs of the couch.

By the time people stopped over for Roy's goodbye, there wouldn't be anything left because Andy would have eaten it all. We could hear water running downstairs, cupping into Andy's hands and splashing over his face, trying to wash out the pits in his skin. Roy and I kept silent, waiting for the faucets to turn off. If he woke, Bo would scream that he was a free man, and we might have to listen to them argue for hours.

"Come with me," Roy said. He had lowered his head, all but his lips, back into the bathwater. I stood up to go to the AA meeting. Roy's head came crashing out of the water, his shoulders then his whole body surrounded by a cloud of steam as it rose into the air.

"I'll think about it," I said. "When I get back from the meeting." And when I looked, the steam rose to cover the shape of his mouth, even his eyes. I could only see his outline, floating in the air. I had seen his face almost every day of my life. Turning to leave, I saw his flailing legs rising on the rope swing into the sky twelve years before. It seemed he would keep rising, but then I remembered the tumbling through the air and crashing into the water. The rope swung back into my hand, and I waited as the ripples flattened out and vanished, but he still did not rise. The place where he had entered was flat and oily black, the windless air around the small pond was utterly silent, as if he had never been there, which made his head bursting out of the water seem like a miraculous arrival of some person I had never known.

It made sense on the way to the meeting, when I rested behind the bank on Commercial Street warming my hands over the air vent, that Florida was a place where you would always be warm. I could not have known that Roy was dying from a disease I might have caught myself, for I had been there, in all the same places, using the same needles. I remember him passing the needle to me—one time I did not take it may have been the time, or the time the needle broke off in his arm or the time he dropped it on the ground and it snapped or I held it in my hand

and thought of nothing at all but the blank gray plaster wall and closed my eyes and passed out. Any of these could have been the time.

We had, all along, hoped for an end with the sting in the arm and the warmth spreading through the body like an orange glow, a direct tap from the sun, and the long slow liquid burn of the scotch or 151 sliding down the throat setting the body loose into a night the mind would not recall. All I knew those last times we went out together dressed in nothing but T-shirts and jeans in the winter, strutting down the block to the bar, was that my skin glowed a powerful red—impervious, my muscles surging with heat. Not even the bouncer's fist three hours later would change that. When the fist slammed, I fell back through the cotton flakes tumbling out of the sky. I fell through the air for hours, it seemed, my face stinging, and landed not on the icy pavement but in a warm, black pool where I could truly rest.

I started running back to the apartment away from the meeting, slipping through the snow and stumbling up the icy steps of the building to tell Roy I would go with him. I came through his bedroom door and rushed back to find that he had already gone, walked down the hill to catch an earlier bus. Andy had eaten the first two batches of cookies and cooked more. His cheeks were filled with dough when I came into the kitchen. Bo hadn't moved from the couch. He was sleeping off the afternoon, so he could go back out that evening. Andy would nurse him back to health and see him out the door so they could fight about it five hours later.

It was a good thing, I decided while sitting at the table eating the cookies next to the warm oven, that Roy had left on the earlier bus and walked down by himself, because no one except Andy and me had come to see him off. I would wait for the spring, until he wrote to give me his address, and by then I would have a job, money—I could fly down to visit. He would know people, be settled right in. Then I might decide to start a new life under the sun and palms. Play tennis, swim.

Richard and Keith said they would stop by after work, but they never did. Andy and I saw them at the meeting the next day, but we didn't talk about Roy. When I walked home that evening, I knew the back room would be empty and the front room would have a little sunlight left—enough so I could take off my gloves and push the button that started the kerosene heater. After the low orange glow spread across the filament, I didn't mind waiting in the cold room watching my breath steam across the last of the day's light, because I could anticipate the room warming. Even though it wasn't true, I felt sure Roy was warm. I had seen pictures of people beneath palm trees in Florida, and I suspected I had been wrong to doubt Roy. Maybe the air was always the exact temperature of skin. Every afternoon he would peel an orange in the sun, letting the skin drop into the dry, hot sand. Every afternoon for the rest of the winter I thought of Roy there, and I saw myself there, too, in the white flame of the heater, in the bubbling air flowing between my eyes and the frosting windows.

After months passed and still there was no mail from him, a hospital in New York called. They had found my address in his pocket. He had taken the bus to Manhattan, where he spent what money he had and what he could steal. After I told myself that I should have gone with him, after I told our mother that he was dead on the street, not in Florida, and after the snow melted and the trees bloomed frantically as if in one day, my mother and I walked across the bridge to the beach in South Portland. It took all morning to cross the bridge and pass from pavement to dirt roads and reach the sand, where I took off my shoes just as I had promised Roy months before—my feet burned so hot I ran straight for the water. I had to think of him another way: slowly removing his sandals under the blue sky and sauntering down to the waterline, walking straight up to his chest in the surf until he had to kick and wave his arms in the lukewarm sea. He would turn around and face the brown legs running up and down the beach. I looked back to my mother, who had sat down in the sand to watch me. My feet leapt over the shallow wash, smarting from the sharp stones beneath. I reached deeper until I could not lift my legs high enough. On the last step I dove without expecting to see him in the vast, cold green which pushed back against me toward the sky. But it seemed possible as I rose for air that Roy, too, would crash up amidst the windblown ripples ignited by the sun into a field of tiny refractions.

After my mother and I first heard about Roy's death and walked down Commercial Street, down Fore Street and out to the bridge, my mother walking in front, two of her steps to one of mine, her red cotton dress blowing sideways in the wind passing down along the Fore River, I expected the sidewalk to open up and swallow us. She reached her hand up into the wind to gather her long, gray hair that splayed out like a fan before the sun and pulled it down beneath her jacket. I could see her hair, just as I saw it a year later spread evenly out across the white sheet of the bed where I found her in the apartment, her hand on the telephone and her mouth open. I knew her heart was weak, but we did not know how weak and we did not know when it would give. Now, a year later, I still have her ashes in the metal jar hidden at the back of the closet.

She first taught me, dancing, eyes closed in the front room in her nightgown twenty years ago, that the city as we saw it outside the window, shining in rows of streets down the hill, could be rearranged and melted into a handheld ball of fire by a simple, delicate turn of her wrist. It seemed true as the humid air filled with whiskey and stale rotting vegetables, the front of her nightgown swaying around her chest as she danced, that she could change the face of everything I knew with her waving, magical arms, and I would be able to touch the air before my face just as I could the water in the sea, and we could walk through the evening as if on the ocean floor, the three of us, through a city of drowning people.

She tried to save Roy and me from this city years later, when she was sober and we had fallen into her life, still living there in the apartment with her. She came home one day to find Roy passed out and naked under the kitchen table, the needle hanging out of his arm. She had to kick us out; she couldn't watch it happen, she said.

When we were young our mother came home from work six or seven hours late and riding in someone else's car. I lay back in bed and stared at the ceiling, but Roy waited at the window at the front of the apartment. I heard the chair push back as he stood up, the padding of his twelve-year-old heels down the hall to the door, and by the time I reached the front window, he was down below pulling our mother away from the man who had brought her home. The man reached out and grabbed Roy's shirt. My mother, startled and tumbling forward, pounded her fists on the man's shoulder. This man could have lifted the two of them, one in each hand, and tossed them. With one twitch of his mustache he threw his arms up in the air while yelling at her. I couldn't hear until I reached my forefinger out and pressed against the window. By that time he was driving away. Roy led her up the stairs, four flights, to our apartment. I stood in the hall as they stumbled inside. Roy took her into the bathroom and rested her on the tub.

"Go back to bed," he shouted at me before slamming the door. In moments I could hear her retching and the water running. I backed away from the door into the room Roy and I shared and sat down on the edge of the bed. An hour later he walked in and lay down on top of the covers. I moved out into the living room and sat in front of the television watching the helicopters on the news descend onto the roofs in the country my father had traveled to. My mother had risen from her stupor and stood in the hall watching from a distance as the people on the roof reached up their hands. She said so often that he would never return from this place that when he did arrive at the door a year later, green bag in hand, I waited for him to speak and move before I would believe he was real.

"It's your father," he said, and I let him through the door. Of course I remembered his face, the line of his jaw and lips, but as he sat down opposite my mother, and I stood behind her, I could see that he was not there with us, not in his eyes the same person. He left that afternoon for good, and it seemed in the following years that the person walking through the door that one day had been a ghost or someone only I had seen—Roy had not been there and my mother refused to talk about it. As far as she was concerned, he never came back, and I began to dream of him still on a roof reaching up toward the sky thousands of miles away, just the side of his face visible to us on the TV screen. For several weeks after seeing him, I climbed up to the flat roof of our apartment building and looked up to the sky knowing that nothing would lower from the clouds to lift me up and away. Still I climbed on top of a vent and lifted my hands up, stretching my fingers as I had seen the people do on the screen, when the men in the door of the helicopter were reaching down.

By contacting the military I found his address five years ago. Yesterday morning I pressed my lips against my wife Angela's neck, and for the first time I drove north an hour to find him down a little road in a two-room house with a stovepipe and white, peeling clapboards. I parked down the street waiting for him to come home. Toward dusk, as the light filtered down through the pines, his old truck pulled into the driveway and he stepped out. I thought I would tell him about my mother passing away and ask if he wanted to come with me to drop her ashes into the ocean, but my hands remained gripped to the steering wheel. I fell asleep sitting there as the moon rose above the dark woods, and in the morning I was still there as he stepped out of the front door rubbing his eyes. He shifted from one leg to another and looked up at the sky and I drove away.

I have been at the beach today with my mother sprinkling what is left of her over the waves she loved to watch for hours in the afternoon as we sat together not speaking these last few, peaceful years. I stood in the surf this time, waist deep in my long pants and bare feet as the green curls slapped against my stomach and splashed up into my face. If the waves were human they would mistake the ocean, as they rose briefly up, for their own kingdom.

I can feel the sand grinding between my toes and the sun long set still beating down on the tops of my hands as I tiptoe through our apartment tonight. Angela is sleeping, unaware not only of my presence but of my mother's death just days ago, of Roy, and of many of the things that have happened to me. Her bare stomach, rounded and stretched with new life, rises and falls beneath my fingertips. I touch my lips to hers and close my eyes. She is so tired that she does not wake, and I remember touching other lips—women at night before we had even spoken and my father's, the night before he left for the war, resting against mine, when I pretended to be asleep.

Angela still plays four times a week. The cello leans cold and quiet against the wall, the wires taut waiting for her callused fingers. I have sat in the audience and watched as she closed her eyes in the quartet and ran the bow over the wires and it sang. I run my hand over her side and watch her closed lids—she is long and hard like a fish, silent like the cello, until her eyes open and I see all the people I have known floating in her black pupils shining in the dim, fluorescent streetlight. She curls close and I bend down to meet her lips searing hot with sleep and dreams. My mind spins wildly, thoughts, phrases, and words spilling, and I am trying to memorize this person—the way she smells and whispers at night, and what she wants me to say and do so that I can see happiness in her face. She pulls away and whispers as I pull off my wet clothes to climb in bed that my lips taste of salt. I press my mouth against her neck and lay my fingers over her stomach. She wants to know where I have been to grow so piercing cold to the touch, as I pull closer, her skin against mine, and I whisper back that I have been out at the beach, swimming.

The Submariners

After work I walked through the middle of the island by the clusters of three-story gray shingled houses along the southeastern shore and arrived at the Abernathys' during the time of day when Grandma held lessons for Hadley. The Senator didn't look up from his paper as Grandma played the piano by resting her hands on top of mine. We opened books on Matisse, Chagal, Picasso, and others. I saw nothing but strange shapes, but she told us that alteration of reality into new forms created a beauty more true than what I could see with my own eyes. I looked out the window and watched the wind moving the pines before a storm, and the clouds gathering and separating.

Hadley and I made our own drawings and showed them to Grandma, who was baking or fiddling around the house before dinner. Hadley bent her head over the paper, her blond hair falling down to cover her face. Her forehead creased as she pushed down so hard on a pastel that it constantly broke in half.

"It's almost time for dinner," Grandma said and asked, as always, if I wanted to stay. I thought of my mother, though, and said I would come another time.

"I'm not hungry," Hadley said, and stomped down the stairs and off the back porch.

"Make sure she comes back for dinner," Grandma told me as I followed.

Before I could leave, Senator Abernathy looked up from his paper and called my name. "That father of yours, in the reserves, right? Is he over there yet?" he said without removing the pipe from his mouth.

"He is supposed to go soon," I lied and thought of the gunfire and jungle I had seen on the news at night.

Grandfather nodded. "Good thing. We need some good men over there the way things are going. You should come sailing with Hadley and me someday. That girl won't lift a line." He made me promise Saturday afternoon, before his guests arrived.

Hadley and I walked to the northwest point, where we had spent hours together—no one could find us there, on a moss-covered rock that formed a natural seat facing upriver toward Wiscasset and the dense, lonely center of the state, where my father and my uncles, cousins, and I had gone deer hunting among the logging roads.

"I want to live here in the winter. We could both work for your father," she said. I tried to picture her narrow arms hauling the traps over the side, and her pale fingers digging into the chum bucket, lifting out fish guts and heads, mussels and clams to stuff the bag, and then at the end of the week her climbing into the wetsuit to dive for lost traps and moorings.

"Your family," I said. "They won't let you."

"Them!" She pounded her knee with her fist. "I wish I could just stay here." Hadley grabbed my hand. "I don't want to go anywhere—not home, not to that school. Anywhere!" When she raised her face, her eyes burned red with a rage I couldn't understand. She had smudged her yellow sweater on the moss. "I haven't seen my parents in over a year," she moaned. "Now I don't even want to see them."

"You have your grandparents."

"They're so busy in Washington. I see them Christmas Day if I'm lucky."

"In the summer."

"In the summer I get to go to all their cocktail parties. Grandma is always trying to teach me something—make me better."

She was scheduled to start a new school in the fall as an entering sophomore. The boarding school where she had lived since she was eight only went to the ninth grade. Her parents ran a manufacturing company with plants in various parts of the world. She rarely saw them or her brothers, who were attending other schools, one of them in England. Her grandparents owned a house in Boston near her school, though they had been living in Washington most of the year. This was the first summer of Grandfather's retirement from the government. He might have more time, I thought.

She let go of my hand and stood up. Muscles stretched along her thigh as she leaned forward against a tree.

"What do you see when you're underwater?"

I didn't want to talk about work. She waved her hand upriver and then out to sea past the lighthouse.

"It's too dark to see down there, even with a light."

Just then, fifteen yards off the rocks, a seal's head popped up.

His glassy black eyes shifted as his whiskers twitched, and he seemed like a bald human treading water. He vanished just as suddenly, leaving no trace except a tiny swirl of water.

I still didn't understand why she was upset. All winter I dreamed of having a father like hers—it wouldn't matter if I never saw him, I thought, as long as he sent me off the island in the winter to Hadley's life. I saw my father every day, and it still felt to me as though he lived on the other side of the world.

"I want to go down there," she said as she pulled two or three tiny bottles of airline booze from her pocket. She uncapped one and slugged it down, wiping her mouth with the back of her hand. I had never seen her drink before. My older cousins drank, and I had tried it but didn't like the taste or the effects—I got sick before drunk.

"You want one?"

I shook my head, so she downed another as if it were orange juice.

"Where'd you get those?"

"A friend gave me a stash before I came to Maine this summer."

I didn't want to know if her friend was a boy.

As a child my father had worked out to sea on cod boats, so when we left at five in the morning in the summer and on the weekends in the winter to pull the traps or dive for urchins (the factories extracted the roe and shipped it to Japan), he was not forcing me into situations that might seem cruel. When I rose to the surface he was there in moments to pluck me out of the cold—I never doubted that I could rely upon him. I would often come down with bronchitis, the result, my father and I both knew, not of the cold but of the inherited weak chest from my mother and her family. I never once heard him complain or blame me in any way for what I could not prevent, and he never once forced me back out to do work before the sickness had receded and I was ready again.

On Monday we rose at five in the morning, and I baited the traps as we motored toward the pots, the boat rumbling up and down the swells, the horizon bursting into view and vanishing again. We hauled the traps in the mornings and dove for urchins in the afternoons. As the sun rose, I leaned over and grabbed the buoy's handle, hauling it up through the winch. The winch motor started to whine as the rope leading down into the dark tensed and the boat leaned. Green musty salt mixed with diesel as the smell of decaying fish bait rose into my nose. In moments the lattice and netting emerged out of the green and splashed into the blue sky, the red and black creatures inside flapping their limbs, their tiny mouths drowning on air. My father's heavy brows drooped over the eyes that I rarely saw. His thick brown arms clutched the traps and released them again moments later. After five hours, after all the traps had been checked and their valuable, sprawling contents saved, we motored to the Cat Ledges, because it was a calm day to dive for urchins. It was my day to go down. He would go the next time.

I could see the light above and the outline of my father's head leaning over the side of the boat watching me. Seen through the water, he had no face, only a blank, pale flap of skin. Either he watched for my safety or to see how I worked. I didn't know. After filling the net with the spiny, fist-sized creatures, I rose to the surface, where he took the catch and handed me a fresh net.

As we headed home at dusk, he said nothing, standing behind the wheel. We never spoke unless he needed to tell me to do something I had either forgotten to do or had not learned, so when he spoke it was always an indication of my failure. I was supposed to remember, and I was supposed to learn by watching him. When he called for me to come take the wheel, I thought something was wrong, but he just walked to the stern, sat down on the transom, and looked across the bay like a tourist. He took an envelope out of his pocket and held it over the water but did not drop it.

The next morning we dove for traps my uncle had lost in a storm. He tossed the anchor as I climbed into my mask and tank. Even in the summer I wore a dry suit with a wet suit beneath, and I dreaded the thought of the opaque, shifting green swallowing the weak streams of early sunlight. I had seen pictures of clear water in the south where people swam in bathing suits above the sandy bottom as if floating in air.

As I dropped into darkness with only the short beam of my light to mark the way, I saw a long white form rising toward me like a ghost from below. My heart did not stop pounding until I touched the object, felt the metal under my hand, and knew that it had once stood in someone's kitchen. The more mud I churned the less I could see around me until I was only searching with my gloved hands for the wooden slats of the traps. My eyes raced around the six or seven inches I could see in front of the light, expecting any moment to find the green eyes of some creature coming toward me. Sensing something behind, I flipped around and shined the light on an entire school of mackerel swarming through the beam, their mouths open and tails flicking faster than my eyes could follow.

The traps were not there. A rope tied to my belt connected me to the boat. Normally I would follow this line back to the surface, but this time I reached around and untied the rope and headed west, swimming toward the island, following the compass on my watch. I was only 150 yards from shore. After ten minutes I rose to the surface and looked back to see my father climbing into his diving gear and preparing to tumble off the stern and look for me. I took off my mask so I could see better as he fumbled with the tank. I had never seen him so unsteady. I continued swimming, and by the time I reached the shore and climbed up on the rocks to stand there in my wet suit, he had surfaced again, too, and was standing on the stern looking down into the water. In our black dripping suits we must have looked like amphibians. I wanted him to think I was still down there, cold and wide-eyed like a mackerel—dead and trapped underwater forever because of him.

Walking home with my gear, I began to feel guilty, but it was too late, I told myself. That night I stayed in my room listening to him and my mother walking around the kitchen. I stared at the door waiting for it to burst open and his angry face to appear.

Later, after changing for supper, I came into the kitchen to find my father, still in his fishing gear, sitting in a chair holding the same envelope. My mother sat across from him watching the envelope rise slightly and tap the surface of the table. The food sat cooling on the stove.

I knew enough not to ask, but I saw on the envelope the emblem of the United States military, and my heart pounded, my mind raced with what I would tell Grandfather the next day.

Without saying a word, my father handed the envelope to my mother, who tucked it in her dress and rose to serve the food.

"Just eat as you are tonight," she said. "The meal's getting cold."

"I'm not going," he said. My mother and I stared at the floor. Obviously he had been thinking about it for a while. "Not a war like this." That was it. My mother served the food and we ate in silence.

By the time I woke in the morning, the day I was supposed to sail with the Abernathys, I could only hear one set of footsteps. In my anxiety about being punished, I had forgotten that he was leaving, and when I finally swung the door open and walked boldly into the kitchen, my mother looked up from the stove shaking her head.

"He's gone."

For a moment I thought: "To the war," but then I remembered and pictured him behind bars in the military jail. A criminal.

On Saturday, sitting on the Hinkley Pilot thirty-five, my eyes raced over the halyards, winches, and tiller, the mahogany polished and varnished to a warm brown. I had never been on a sailboat, the wood bright instead of painted, the deck long, narrow, and far off the water.

Hadley sat with her back to the cabin, her brown legs thrust out toward me along the seat as Grandfather leaned over the sails on the deck, his pants separating from his shirt so that the tops of two big white hams appeared. Hadley saw me staring and turned.

"Grandpa!" she yelled, rolling her eyes. He craned his head around, ashes flying out of his pipe. "Pull up your pants!" He reached around and gave a quick tug which changed nothing.

"The best way to learn is to start right in." He handed me the tiller.

I knew about wind and tide. On the lobster boat my father used a sail in back to stabilize us in heavy winds and rolling seas. Here the sails were used to move us forward.

"You've sailed before," he said.

"No," I told him. I made a point of it. "No, I haven't."

"So your father's still waiting to go over?"

"He was just called up," I almost shouted but then tried to

remember what I had said in the beginning of the week to make sure I had not contradicted myself. I couldn't remember, but Grandpa's expression didn't change, so I assumed everything was all right. He slapped his hand on my back.

"You'll have to come to dinner tonight to celebrate."

As the wind rose, Grandfather took back the helm.

Wind against the tide, I thought. Waves crashed over the starboard bow and sprayed the cockpit.

"Hadley, come down from there!" Grandfather shouted.

She stood forward on the deck gripping one of the stays as the boat pitched up and down. The whitecaps crashed against the hull and flew up in the air around her face, turning her skin a glistening mahogany.

Grandfather called again for her to come down. Otherwise he would have thought then of reducing the amount of sail. I prayed that she would resist him and that the wind would grow with his anger until she would be swept overboard. I would go over after her. On his third call she snapped her face back to look at us, her eyes narrow, and scornful. She did come down to sit safely braced against the cabin, but by then the wind had changed direction and gusted. The boat heeled over until the rail was buried.

"Hold this!" Grandfather yelled and jumped forward to loosen the halyard on the genoa so we could lower the sail. Hadley sat down on the leeward side of the cockpit. She turned her eyes toward the water as it flowed into her lap. She turned her angry face to me, as if I had just dumped a bucket of water on her. Grandfather tripped and fell against the seat. We had blown down, come up into the wind, and lost momentum. There was nothing I could do at the helm. Grandfather loosened the sheets, which set the boom jumping and kicking as the main lowered and stuck halfway. The genoa sheet caught and would not loosen; the sail filled with air again and started to pull us over.

"It won't come down!" Grandfather shouted to the bow but did not move. I thought we would tip over, though the heavy keel would prevent that. The real danger, Grandfather knew, lay in the Cat Ledges twenty-five yards downwind. He kept staring forward. Hadley stared at him, her eyes narrow and red with rage. I climbed past the mast and found the genoa. The sheet had jammed itself against a broken stanchion. Bracing myself against the gunwale, I slid down the leeward side of the deck until I reached the line, pulled my father's knife out of my pocket, and cut the rope in three passes. The sail exploded flapping into the air and the boat slowly righted itself.

Grandfather unfroze from his position and started the motor. Without sail, the day seemed relatively calm. My father and I had survived ten times that force. We motored home the rest of the way in silence, Hadley wrapped in her jacket and Grandfather chewing on his unlit pipe, obviously ashamed that he had lost control, and possibly upset that I had been the one to rescue us. I had wanted to do the heroic thing, but suddenly I regretted drawing attention to myself at all. When we reached the mooring, Hadley suddenly stood up, dropped her jacket, and dove into the water.

"What's the matter with her?" Grandfather said to the water. Then to me: "Would you grab what is left of that line you cut?"

I watched for Hadley to rise, but there was only the ripple where she had entered and darkness below. Grandfather turned away and seemed to forget her. A seagull swooped down and glided over the water, hunting for fish, and in moments she sprang to the surface gulping for air. I looked away, grabbed the cut line, and handed it to Grandfather, who threw it in the bottom of the dinghy, and we rowed ashore, his pipe inches from my nose.

We put the equipment not stored on the boat into the boathouse, and I ran down to the water to find Hadley standing in the seaweed shivering and soaked, with her eyes closed. I took off my jacket and rested it on her shoulders. She handed it back to me, though, and walked ahead of me in her bare feet on the rough path.

I stopped walking. "Do you want me to come with you or not?" I yelled ahead. I expected her, though I didn't know why, to keep walking, not look back, and never to say another word to me. She took another two steps and turned around to run back.

"I thought you were coming to dinner?" she asked, straining to sound natural.

"I am," I said and took her hand, and we walked. She still shivered, but I knew not to comfort her.

After dinner that night we moved into the living room for backgammon. Hadley and her grandfather played every night while Grandma read next to the fire, sipping from her coffee. Smoke rose from his pipe, obscuring his brown eyes and whiskered face.

"She's a shaker," he said, apparently to me. "Watch this. It's all shakes right from the beginning."

On the third roll she threw double sixes. Grandfather sank back on the couch and puffed harder. "Hadley, Hadley. Ohhh, ohh."

Later the grandparents settled down to Bach and the *New York Times*, three days delayed by the journey north, while Hadley brought me to the second floor. We sat on a couch before a long window and looked across the bay to the Knubble lighthouse, which flashed twice in quick succession. The beam darted across the dark water and disappeared. Hadley leaned forward and pulled on the bottom piece of wood, below the drawers, on an old chest.

"This is Grandma's secret hiding place," she whispered and pulled out a leather box and a folder full of papers. She handed the box to me and opened the folder.

"Open it," she said.

I undid the latches and lifted the lid to find necklaces and compartments containing golden rings. Hadley tilted the sheet toward the moonlight. "Number fourteen," she said and craned her face over the box, her cheek inches from my lips so that I could smell spring on the island. She raised a necklace that sparkled gold in the light, and rested it around my neck.

"It looks perfect for you," she said and giggled before backing up to the window so she could read the sheet. Her face was swallowed in darkness. I could only see the outline of her narrowing torso and the outside curve of her new breasts tapering down to her waist.

In the morning my mother's sister came over from her house to help with chores, and I was expected to take on the duties of the man, according to my mother. I did not want to ask what these duties included. She seemed to imply that I should already know. My father's boat was hauled by his brother-in-law and cousin, so I was not expected at such a young age to start out to sea on my own. Because of the year's bad catch, I was not even asked to serve as a deckhand on my uncle's boat—he had his son for that. I rose early and shadowed my mother around the house as I would my father when I was meant to learn a certain skill. After the third morning she turned on me: "Shoo!" she shouted. "Go, busy yourself." So I left.

On Wednesday I traveled by boat and hitch to visit my father at the local base, where a guard ushered me into a windowless room containing two chairs and a table. My father sat on one side and I on the other. The guard watched us through a window in the door. Here, for the first time, there was nothing for us to do but talk—no work, and I was faced with the dull eyes that focused over my shoulder on the blank, gray wall behind. I waited for him to bring up the incident of my swimming ashore. When I stole a glance at his face, I could see that he had other things on his mind. Somehow this made me more afraid. I had expected a long talk.

"Your mother. How is she?"

"Good."

"You take care of your mother," he said.

I nodded but was afraid to answer—what was I supposed to do?

"They take my boat out of the water?"

"Yes, sir."

"Go check on it for me, every other day."

For several minutes that felt like hours we sat in silence before he stood up and said: "Run on back. Don't leave your mother alone."

I didn't move right away. I didn't understand anything about where the military had asked him to go, only that I wanted him to go.

"Hurry up," he barked. Still I didn't move, so he stood up, shaking his head, and left the room. Only when I heard him and the guard walking down the hall did I stand and leave.

I spent the next morning following my mother around the house again before she said, "You're driving me crazy. Go out there and play or something. I don't care what you do."

Now I was free every day. Hadley and I wandered through her house. Her hips swayed and her right hand bunched into a fist with a heightened tension and anger beyond what I had known in previous summers. I followed her into the living room, and Grandma called from upstairs: "Hadley, David."

"God." Hadley rolled her eyes. "Why don't you go see what she wants?" I started up the stairs as Grandfather, who was eating lunch with four or five visitors out on the front porch, called for Hadley.

"Tell her if you two want to come up, I have a new box of pastels," Grandma said from the top of the stairs. She seemed sad, and I felt sorry for her.

I returned downstairs, where I lingered near the doorway peering at Grandfather and his guests. Hadley stood before them with her hands clasped behind her back.

"David." Grandfather motioned to me, and I stepped into the sunlight to meet the four men. "David, your father been called up yet?" I had told him so in the sailboat.

"Yes, he's over there now," I lied, trying to stand like Hadley—at attention.

"Where is he, exactly?" one of the men in a red golf shirt asked.

"Da Nang," I blurted out, having seen the name on a map, saying it "Day Nan."

"Very good," the man said and smiled. "Day Nan."

Grandfather pointed his sandwich at two of the men, introducing them as government people from other states, Senators like Grandfather, I later learned. He moved his sandwich to the left and told me the names of the other two, who were described as businessmen. When asked what my father did in the war, I replied, because it seemed like the right answer, that he carried a gun, an M-16. Two of the men closed their eyes and smiled.

"Mr. Franklin builds helicopters," Grandfather said.

"I'm sure he flies in those," I said quickly.

"I'm sure he does," the man replied, his mouth still full of lettuce. He caught a few pieces that had fallen out and carelessly tossed them back in his mouth.

"They didn't have these air taxis in my time. We had to walk," Grandfather jeered them. He lifted a stringy piece of lettuce from the edge of his bread and dropped it over the side of the porch.

The man sitting closest to him, who seemed the oldest, rested his sandwich down on his knee. "I knew you back then, Bob. You needed the exercise."

Hadley backed away, and so did I, but I could not take my eyes off the man who built helicopters.

I took the boat over each week as my mother requested but would spend the time reading Grandma's books on shore instead of hitching to the base to see my father. I knew that Hadley was learning at a faster rate and I wanted to keep up. I also knew that my father was sure to mention my absence to my mother, who visited him on a different day, but he never did. I lied to her, saying my visits to him were fine, and she never pressed for more.

I wondered how far Hadley wanted me to go there in the open at the east end beach. She did not seem to realize that the previous summer's bathing suit stretched across her chest and behind. I had always spread sunscreen on her back, but now my hands lingered and explored along her legs and thighs. Lying on her stomach, she opened her eyes halfway and raised her head just an inch. My hands froze on the backs of her legs as she turned her head in my direction and sighed. I could smell the whiskey from her breath float through the warm air.

I rubbed every inch of exposed skin three times or more until the sun had fallen below the line of trees over the hill by the Tafts' house. I sat back and she sat up on her knees. We heard Grandfather yelling from the porch above. It was cocktail hour, and her presence was needed among the adults. She sat for a moment longer, staring with drooping eyes at a place in the sand behind me. Her grandfather's voice called again, louder this time and more insistent. Hadley's eyes fell blank, her jaw stiff. She rose and left me.

Three weeks after my father had left, my mother sat down at the table and told me he had changed his mind and decided to go to the war. He had given in. It seemed to me that I had been triumphant. Maybe I had hurt him enough to make him go, and part of me wanted revenge on him for sending me down underwater all those times. It was because of him that I had to pretend to be part of Hadley's world and that I had to spend each long winter without her.

In a few short weeks we received a letter from him, and it turned out that I had been right after all. That afternoon I sat next to Hadley as she read from a magazine in the living room. I saw Grandfather talking with one of his friends from the island on the porch, and I wandered around the edge of the bookcase, watching their faces through the old warped glass. They both leaned forward, elbows on knees, their backs to the ocean, and spoke in hushed tones. I tried to act as if I were just walking by. Grandfather did not look up as I slowed and looked at his sagging gray jowls.

"Mr. Abernathy," I said softly. Both men stopped talking and looked at me. "I got a letter," I said, "from my father today, from Da Nang." I pronounced it Day Nan again.

"Da Nang," he snapped and then caught himself. He closed his eyes and shook his head quickly before waving me forward until he could reach my shoulder with his rough hand and shake me a little.

"All right, that's good," he said with a slight grimace. "You stand by your old dad, you hear me? He's going to need you."

"Yes, sir," I replied. He slapped me on the back, which meant I was to go back in the house.

After dinner one night Hadley called me at home. My mother held the phone out for me. Hadley's grandparents were out and had left her behind. She wanted me to come over right away. Her voice cracked and her breaths were short, so I sprinted out the door, offering no explanation to my mother.

"David!" she called after me, but she was too tired from the housework she never asked me to help her with.

I ran across the island through the damp, cool smell of pines and moss and up the steep steps to the sight of the sun's last light on the ocean. Hadley sat with her knees curled up and her face lowered into them.

"My grandfather's mad at me," she said. "He thinks I spend too much time with you, that you're over here too much for my good."

"Your grandmother or your grandfather?"

"My grandfather," she hissed and jumped off the railing onto the porch. I pictured her grandfather's eyes.

"What have I done?"

"Nothing!" she yelled, not at me nor in my defense, but in her own defense. We went inside, where a fire blazed from Grandfather's teatime. She strutted back and forth in front of the fire, clenching and unclenching her fists. Suddenly she turned to me with tears pouring out of her eyes and her cheeks burning red.

"He called me a little slut, and Grandma just stood there! She didn't say anything," she screamed and picked up a glass from the table by Grandfather's chair. I smelled the booze from five feet away. "I had to tell them I got it from you. I'm sorry, David. They were going to . . . I don't know what they were going to. Grandfather was so angry I had to tell them it was you who gave it to me."

"That you got what from me?" I asked and then I knew that they had found her stash of little bottles, or worse: they had found her drunk.

She swallowed more and put the glass back down before crumbling onto me, wrapping her arms around my neck. In a moment without letting go of each other we sat down in front of the fire.

She dug her fingers into my back as if afraid I might run away any minute.

"I don't know what's wrong with me," she whimpered.

"You can come live with me," I said. "With my mother and me."

She did not respond. I did not recognize the red glow in her eyes as she pulled me to her chest, where I rested my cheek and listened to her heart. She spread her legs around me and ran her hands through my hair as I had seen people do in movies, and we seemed as old as those people, though it also seemed as if we would never be that old.

It was not clear if they had come back early from dinner or stopped by between cocktails on the way to dinner.

"Get your hands off her!" Grandfather screamed, picking me up by the hair and dragging me out the back door. Grandmother stood in the front doorway silently watching. I walked calmly down the back stairs under the hail of his threats: I should never come back to the house, I should never call. I walked all the way across to the other side of the island. My mother was in the kitchen when I returned and stood before her, shock but no tears on my face.

"What happened?" she asked, standing up with some difficulty, but I could not answer. I did not have to. She had known all along about Hadley and had kept it a secret from my father. Finally she draped a blanket over my shoulders, more for comfort than for warmth, settled me down on the couch, and stood above stroking my hair, not saying a word. These moments of love from her were always doled out in secrecy from my father. Now that he was away, I could let tears flow down my face shamelessly and she could sit above and ruin me for a life of working on the ocean.

No call came from Hadley nor her grandparents. I determined not to go over there until she tried to contact me. At first I thought the whole misunderstanding would be cleared up right away. Then I heard at the post office that she was headed off island earlier than usual. My mother asked me to do chores that I would start and not be able to complete—an indolence I had never known came over me, and I feared the winter that would leave me with nothing but my own thoughts.

On several occasions I started across the island to visit Hadley, but each time it occurred to me that one of them—at least Grandma—would have called if Hadley had told them the truth. And I was sure she would tell them if I only waited. I didn't let myself believe for a moment that she would sacrifice me so easily. When my cousins had been caught drinking, nothing bad happened to them at all. I was sure that Grandma would be the one to call. First she would make amends for her husband's behavior, then she would make amends for Hadley and express gratitude that Hadley had at least one honest friend. Despite the lies I had told about my father, I thought of myself as an upright person and imagined that all the boys Hadley knew in her winter life just tried to get her drunk so they could take advantage of her. I refused to believe that I was not somehow superior to the people she knew in the winter, possibly because I feared the obvious: that I was expendable. If I wasn't better-looking, or more intelligent, or richer, I must have stronger character, and so I would not call—I would prove to her how strong I could be.

I was chopping wood on the hill above the house when I saw the two men in uniform motoring across the bay in a Coast Guard boat. I didn't understand at first why I could not move. Even when I saw them dock in front of our house it did not occur to me what they might want. I ran for them instinctively, having no idea what I would do or say. I had the general sense that I must make them turn back across the water. I stumbled on a root and flew onto the ground. By the time I stood and began running again, it was too late.

Our back door opened and their broad green shoulders stood inside. My mother stood in front of them, boxed in. Her hand clutched at a sleeve and she was falling. I called out—for a moment I didn't think he would catch her. Her hands flew to my face and pulled my head into her body. I had to wrap my hands around her waist to hold both of us up. "Go!" my mother screamed to the men, to their hands.

He was not gunned down in combat as I had imagined being able to tell Grandfather but in an accident on the base. That was my first thought—how it would sound as I announced it to Grandfather, and how he would console me on our next sailing trip; and then, as I realized I never would tell the Abernathys, I felt as though I were underwater, deep in the green with no wet suit or flashlight, my skin turning numb from the cold. Staring at the water, I thought I might see my father rise out of the green chop wearing his mask and dark suit, emerging like a seal just offshore to bob in the waves and keep his eyes on me. The air squeezed out of my lungs, and I felt a scream building inside me, but the rage carried no further than my mind, where it would reverberate for years, eventually shaking me to pieces.

I couldn't sleep that night and did not want to go with my mother the next afternoon to seek comfort from her sister, so I stayed in bed and listened to the waves. Someone knocked on the door. I knew it was her without looking, but I rolled over and pulled the curtain aside to make sure. She knocked again and stepped back to look up at my window just as I pulled away. I knew she had come to say goodbye and possibly to apologize, but I hid behind the wall and listened to her call my name because I needed someone to blame for more than she could understand.

Two days after we found out about my father, I walked across the island to the west float and watched Hadley and her grandparents motor off in the boat for the mainland. It was the end of the summer, 1968, and I would never see Hadley nor my father again. Seven years later, I would hear at Grover's Store about her marriage, then, in another two years, about her death in a convertible. The grandparents were still alive then but very old, and they sold the house that had been in their family for three generations. They had no other grandchildren, no one to pass it on to. A younger man, single, and from New York, bought the big house and also the Senator's sailboat. He flew up for weekends to sit on the porch and look out over the water. Sometimes he would sit on the deck of the boat, but he never took it out. Grover said he had no idea whatever of how to sail.

Though I stood behind a tree the afternoon Hadley and her family left for the summer, as they came down to the dock in a trail, I did not think of myself as hiding, and I stepped out into the open as the boat left, driven by Grandfather, to make the trip back to Boston and their winter life. The three of them waved to the half a dozen friends who had come to see them off. I walked further toward the dock because I wanted Hadley to see me before she left. Maybe I sensed that she would not return the following summer or the summer after. I wanted her and all of them to know that my father was dead. I had been waiting to tell them, I realized, in order to believe it myself; now that they were leaving I feared I might never believe it.

The white hull of the Abernathys' boat cut through the calm green surface. I waved harder as a dark patch of ripples crossed their path, a solitary breeze traveling toward shore. As they veered south toward Townsend Gut, Hadley stopped waving. Her eyes met mine, but the boat was reaching a plane, speeding away, and my hand stopped waving, too, as I realized my lips were forming words that could never travel across the water.

Sadness of the Body

It is sown in dishonor;
It is raised in glory.
—1 Corinthians 15:43

In 1968 my uncle was in charge of the body count. He says very few of the bodies had all their parts by the time he found them, and that some of the smaller parts had already been taken as trophies. A dead body, he says, is heavy like a bag of sand. The war, he says, was all about bodies.

We four cousins, my uncle, and his girlfriend sit half nude in a rented vacation cottage drinking iced tea and vodka in the 102 heat. The liquid pours in our mouths and then seeps from our bodies as if it had been poured through sand. When it's this hot and none of us can sleep, we wander around all night looking for cooler places. When it's this hot, the body becomes sad.

What Is the Body?

My uncle says the body is for buying beer. The body is mostly ocean anyway, he says, mostly liquid. It is constantly drowning. My cousins and I have come from all over the country to stay here with him and his girlfriend. At night we can hear the surf, and during the day we hear people yelling as they run and dive into it. We're here on vacation.

Our parents, most of them ten years older than my uncle, the baby of the family, stay in a bigger house just down the beach. My uncle prefers to stay with us, he hates grown-ups, he says.

My mother thinks the body is a way to get to the store. My father thinks the body is a place people work after they're born. What do they know? my uncle says about them.

When we were young we cousins wondered about those people, like the sandman, the tooth fairy, and that late Aunt Sally the family toasted while looking at the ceiling. How they got around? Certain people, we determined for a while, had no need for bodies. When I stayed with my cousins at my grandfather's farm in the middle of the New Hampshire woods, we would often hear an old Model T driving up the road to the front of the house. The car door slammed and apparently someone got out. We all rushed to the window, but there was never anybody there. My grandfather would explain to our petrified faces that we had just heard somebody else's dream.

Word and Body

In his sleep my uncle speaks to himself, going on about people and places we know nothing about.

The word from my uncle's lips in the morning is "hot." So hot that our words seem to melt right after they hit the air. "What did you say?" sounds like the gurgles of a drowning man once it travels across the room, the air is so thick.

Our bodies have very little to say; they have seen it all and could tell us all, if we would listen. We are too busy. The body is a silent sufferer. It knows all the wrong directions, has taken them all before.

My uncle says that he has to use the john and then we should walk to the beach. Then he uses the john and we walk to the beach. One of my cousins spends the whole morning complaining about his body, how it hurts, what it won't do after he put a quart of whiskey down his throat twelve hours ago. At the beach he keels over onto his towel and falls asleep. My uncle drank more, but he starts up the football game; he can do anything to his body and it will obey. A long time ago he made some kind of deal with his body.

Any body, however, will listen to commands for only so long. We are reminded, and if we don't listen, the body leaves us in the cold.

On the beach our bodies are amused that we still enjoy talking about ourselves. Our bodies get restless, listening to us talk, and wander away from each other before long. On the beach playing touch football they talk to each other in sign language, catching up on old news. Muscles form bulges and ridges like bodies within the body trying to get out. Especially with a pink sunburn, they act like they know it all. On either side of the ball, we huddle together. Waiting for the hike, our bodies whisper to each other like ushers.

Only later, driving home with sand dust dried between our toes, do we have a feeling what our bodies have said to each other. I convince myself that it was nothing important—vanity. Body stuff.

Body Parts

The spleen suffers from terminally low self-esteem. It refuses to talk to the rest of the body.

Some parts of the body are like vegetables. The biceps, for instance, could easily be potatoes; the feet, summer squash. When one of these parts falls asleep, I poke it and think: This could be a part of someone else's body.

Vestigial organs are the professors of the body: protective of what they know and jealous of what they can't do. The appendix, for instance, dreams of a life without the body.

My legs are like old lovers who won't forgive each other. They are unfaithful with the legs of other bodies, and are only happy when hidden from each other in a pair of pants.

The soles of the feet were born into a lousy job. Only when the body is prostrate do the soles glimpse what the face generally knows. But the soles of the feet know the world best of all. They are the Atlas of the body, carrying the body's sadness to where it needs to go. Because of the feet, the body knows stories about the ground that it refuses to tell.

In Vietnam my uncle had to organize a separate pile for body parts that had lost their owners. He was instructed to count five body parts as one body and to bury the parts in a grave marked for enemy bodies.

My uncle's parts are growing and shrinking. The skin frowns around the bones in his ass and legs. The skin around his shoulders, arms, and chest sags in the same way, while the stomach has bulged out and turned pale yellow. Certain parts of his body are dying off to save other parts. For people like my uncle, who works with computers, every part of the body except the brain has become a vestigial organ, aching for the past. Our arms and legs remember a day when they were of more vital use, and in some places they still are but not here. You see nothing but blue-veined limbs on these brown beaches.

All the parts of the body are ill equipped for living in the world. In the ocean the fingers turn numb—in ten minutes we are hypothermic. And in the sun our skin turns red and burns into the night. We were meant for some other world.

Where the Body Travels

Usually, what happens is that the body gets in a car and drives somewhere. The body is only happy when it has the hope of traveling somewhere. The body never wants to arrive.

When my uncle stands up this evening, his body frowns at itself. We stand up too, our skin nervously tight around our bones, and follow him out onto the porch, where our bodies seem to wait as if for a ride to take them somewhere.

There is nowhere to go, not even a movie theater or a bar in this little place where people bring their bodies to wade in the sea. Where, walking through the surf, you can have freezing feet and a steaming head at once. It's considered a luxury in our time.

One of the greatest luxuries is travel, but the body often forgets that it is moving through time. Time, however, is ungrateful to the body. The body carries time on its back. Without the body, time could not move, and without movement there would be no time.

From the very beginning, in any case, our bodies knew that time is where they have to go. The ancient creases in the body are just waiting for us to arrive. But when it is this hot with so little wind, the slightest breeze creeping out of the ocean air that brushes quickly against us and disappears promises the body so much more. The body convulses and complains: the body cries sweat through every pore for somewhere else to travel when its time is over. It already feels left behind.

In any case the trouble is pride. Time doesn't care about that, it is so old. Time has traveled through too many bodies to be concerned with loss. Like all ideas, time is a most unfaithful lover.

The Pleasure of the Body

My uncle lies on his stomach as his girlfriend runs an ice cube down his back. The cool liquid collects in the pool at the base of his spine. More than anything, the body loves water. When it's this hot, an ice cube reminds our bodies of when we were fish sitting down at the darkest, coolest part of the ocean.

And we love the sun, the warm rays on our skin after a dark winter. With very few exceptions the world is colder than we are. We love fire for warming our fingertips, but mostly we love the body of fire, the flames. Flames dance with a kind of freedom that the body knows and the mind can only imagine. The body itself is slowly burning.

My uncle, one other cousin, my uncle's girlfriend, and I are sitting in the quiet heat listening to the waves cooling the beach. Our bodies love to believe a good lie. My uncle's girlfriend, seven years younger than my uncle and a mere ten years older than my cousin and I, lies against my uncle's body on the couch and puts the ice cube in her mouth. Her nipples stand up against her tank top and the bottom of her bikini rides up between her legs. My cousin and I stare at her while my uncle lies on his stomach facing the wall. They are from another time. Our bodies tingle at the sight of them, but our minds are afraid.

My uncle suddenly turns on his side facing us, takes his beer off the table, and slowly pours it over her body, soaking her hair, her shoulders, stomach, waist, and legs. She turns on her side also, leaning on one elbow, and with the opposite hand spreads the beer over herself like suntan lotion. Then she props one leg up, keeping the other one straight, and she looks at me. My uncle puts the beer down and reaches down in back between her legs with his free hand. Her eyelids sag but she still stares at me. My cousin stands up and walks to the bedroom. When her eyes close I stand up and walk out onto the porch. I walk halfway down the steps, sit down, and stare at the dark space where the ocean meets the beach. It's night. I pull several pills out of my shirt pocket and plop them in my mouth, washing them down with a can of beer. The pills roll down the back of my throat and scrape their way down to the middle of my body. I sip from the beer again, the cold bite on my tongue in this steamy heat, the cold traveling in a wave down to the center of my body. Lying back in the sand, I wait for the feeling of having no bones. I lift some sand and sift it slowly onto my belly.

The body loves taking off shoes after a long walk, and it loves the first give of a pillow before a nap and the last moments before sleep. After climbing down a mountain, the body loves lowering its face into an icy stream. The body loves ice cream.

The body goes from body to body and sees nothing wrong, only pleasure.

At my grandfather's funeral this summer, mine was the only body that laughed. Laughing is one of the body's favorite ways to get rid of things.

Mind and Body

My uncle is a philosopher of bad ideas. As he goes to the window this morning, he flexes the map of the United States tattooed on his back. Montana bulges out of the shoulder.

When the body wakes it has forgotten everything. This morning my cousin turns to me with a glass of iced coffee, his eyes half open with sleep, and says, "Here . . ." His sleepy mind can't remember my name. At first I think this peculiar, but then it makes sense. Our bodies know what they see—another body.

Later, when our minds scramble to focus on the day, my cousin will no longer seem like just a body with its angles and particular features. It's how our minds gradually clothe our bodies to face the day.

Walking by the upstairs bathroom, I hear a "psssst." Looking in, I see my uncle sitting on the edge of the tub. He holds the top of the long plastic tube toward me. I grab the middle and raise the end to my mouth, placing my thumb over the hole. He flicks the lighter as I inhale, listening to the sizzle of burning grass.

Then: "C'mere," he says from by the window. I walk over (it seems to take forever) and blow the smoke out the window. "Down there," he says. We can see over the fence into the neighbor's lawn, where a young woman leans back in a lawn chair with her top off. She puts her palm on her stomach and spreads her fingers there. "If I were you I would fall in love," my uncle says, resting his hand on my shoulder.

"She's nice," I say.

"Go over there in the nude, and tell her you're in love—that's what I would do."

"I don't know," I say, "if that sounds like such a good idea."

"Whatever you do," he says, running his hand down along a purple scar that stretches from hip to nipple, "Don't waste your time."

In 1969 my uncle's helicopter crashed somewhere in the I Trang, deep in the jungle. He and three other men crawled out of the wreckage and rested their broken bones next to a tree. One of the men lay dead in the helicopter. My uncle collapsed on his stomach, half unconscious, while a Vietcong patrol came out of the brush and shot the two men sitting against the tree.

The other man, lying a foot to the left of my uncle, was stabbed to death with a bayonet. Then the Vietcong soldier jabbed his bayonet into my uncle's side and tore the skin off from the hip to the armpit. My uncle, who was already covered with the blood of his dead friend, did not flinch. The soldier took him for dead and left him there. Six hours later a rescue helicopter picked him up along with the bodies of his friends. He was nearly dead. In a matter of hours, he was home in the United States, his body flown across the Pacific by jet. Weeks later he stood on a platform with the wives of his dead friends and received a medal. It was as if, my uncle has said, the wives were living parts of his dead friends' bodies.

The night after he received the medal my uncle ripped all the stitches out of his side and wandered around San Francisco drunk, blood pouring down his side. A teenage girl found him leaning against the side of a building. She called an ambulance.

"If I were you . . ." my uncle says again. Then he steps into the shower. I can hear the water falling over his body, the long drips racing down his thighs and into the drain.

Body Mistakes

Casey Mills, from years ago, acted like someone who was rich enough to own another body. Young men like my cousins and me who aren't really young anymore and whose bodies don't like our jobs at home often complain that our bodies behave like women.

My uncle shows me something he learned in Vietnam. He slaps his wrist as if it has done something wrong. He inserts the needle and releases the strap. He leans his head back and spreads his arms as if waiting for it to fall from the ceiling: that feeling of more. He doesn't know that I've already learned on my own.

I sit down next to him, drawing in half of what he did, and find the blue line in my arm. Finally, I loosen the strap on my arm, letting the built-up blood rush through my body. The peace falls over my nerves. My body has no choice but to believe the lie. Then eventually, I know, the body starts to believe that it can't live without the lie.

As part of the 1st Cav, my uncle often went on first-light and last-light sweeps over the Mekong Delta. Using the modern version of the Gatling gun or a mounted M-60, the door gunner was ordered to shoot anything that moved, whether it appeared to be a cow, a civilian, or a piece of machinery. Any fallen body was a *kill*, tallied and sent back to Washington as evidence of winning the war.

How many bodies could the enemy have? An endless number, my uncle says. They had an endless number of bodies. That's how they won.

My uncle's girlfriend comes out of the bathroom shaking her head. Everyone else is down at the beach, soaking themselves in the ocean. She has just come back from there and washed the salt off her body in a cold shower. My uncle nods off, tipping over on the couch and falling asleep.

She picks the needle up off the bed. "Help me," she says, grabbing one of his shoulders. I stand up with some difficulty and grab the other shoulder; we drag him into the bedroom and lay him down. Grab the other end, she says, pulling on one of his shirt sleeves. I walk around to her side of the bed and stand next to her. I lean next to her, my arm touching hers, and grab onto his shirt and pull.

"Pull harder," she says. But I'm afraid his arm will come off. "Pull harder," she says again with her eyes clamped shut, and I do. Outside the room she leans on the wall, and then she leans on me in her bikini, sobbing on my neck. The tiny hairs that run down my stomach and vanish into my shorts bristle against her flat, brown stomach. I think I can tell you what it's like for her to lean against my stomach. There's nobody around to stop us, there's no stopping my body. Hunger is a kind of insatiable grief. I watch myself falling down to the floor over my uncle's girlfriend, but worse than that, I watch myself falling down into my uncle's life. Both things are hard to watch.

It is so easy to blame the body for what we do not know, as if it were a scientist who made promises.

History of the Body

We have come a long way. The body never lies. We may rely absolutely on what it says.

The body is history. In the story of time the body is never lost. It is a temporary accretion of incomplete material ideas, nothing more. It is not afraid.

We are afraid because we know nothing about history. We try to find ourselves there but see only darkness. We cannot read the lines in our own faces.

At some point this afternoon my uncle wandered out to the beach and fell asleep in the sun. By nightfall, his body has developed a heat rash across its chest. He squeezes his eyes shut, clenches his teeth, and tries to think about something else. He surrenders to the temptation of the body to itch, digging his fingers into the collarbone and scraping them down to his belly. The rest of his body is momentarily appreciative, but then the itching gets worse. He thrashes at his chest, slapping it with the palms of his hands. He punches himself hard like an animal showing off at the zoo. Then he starts swearing, digging his fingernails into his chest and scraping them down until he draws blood. Some relief comes to his face until his girlfriend takes his arm and pulls it away. He pushes her onto the couch. She puts her head between her knees and asks us to do something for him. He digs his nails back into his forearm, tearing off layers of skin. I stand up from my chair and grab his hands, pulling them toward my body. His nails dig into my wrists and his eyes turn red. Finally he yanks them away from me, walks to the corner of the room, and digs his nails back into his chest.

My cousins and I surround my uncle and drag him down the steps to the beach. We hope to put out the fire, even if just for a moment, that burns in his chest. Low tide forces us to run over half a mile of sand flats and ankle-deep water toward the sound of the surf. My uncle runs ahead, his arms churning through fog as the cousins follow. I stop and watch them go. They shout encouragement and splash each other, their bodies vanishing into darkness, only the breakers marking time across the horizon. After their feet leave the sand, water flows in to erase what their soles have said to the mud.

The Dog Lover

Give not that which is holy to dogs.
—Matthew 7:6

Today my father's playing golf. Not the kind of golf you play on grass but the kind of golf you play in the mind. A blind man's game. He tees off at twelve-thirty, wanders around the house following the same path between tables and chairs, the number of steps between objects memorized, and finishes the eighteenth hole in the kitchen next to the refrigerator at seven over par. I hear his slippers scraping along the hardwood floors, pausing every few seconds for his mind to line up a drive or a putt. Longer pauses indicate rare trouble: the woods maybe, or a sand bunker.

Waiting for him to finish his golf this morning, the one day I visit him each week, I reach down into my bag and pull out a small manual on raising dogs. In my spare time or in the moments before sleep, I think about dogs. One day I would like to raise them professionally. Lexi, the collie that my father gave to me several years ago, wanders into the living room from the kitchen, presses her nose against my thigh, and slowly lowers her hindquarters at my feet. She closes her eyes, but she does not sleep. The growth which originally caused pressure in her neck has spread pain throughout her entire body by now. Her breaths are more like gasps and her chest quivers in anticipation of a relief that does not come. I reach into my pocket and pull out the thermometer. Seven weeks since conception and her stomach has started to bald. She hasn't eaten much of her food the past few days. It's a race between the puppies growing in her uterus and the disease growing in her body. My father's right—if it were not for the puppies, we would have put her to sleep long ago.

When her temperature dips below 100 degrees, it's time for the birth, but I should put the thermometer away, because we are far from that time. I go over the procedure in my head, just in case it does happen early. In the foyer outside my kitchen, the whelping box is readied with layered newspapers and an old blanket. The puppies should come at half-hour intervals. Lexi should do most of the work if she can handle it. Even if she lives to the birthing time, she may die before the pups come out. I'm there to cut the cords, clean up the mess, and make sure none of the puppies get jammed. Old-timers suggest evaporated milk, corn syrup, and egg yolks as a supplement to mother's milk. Watch for puppies scratching the mother. Feed them at three weeks. Wean at five. If she doesn't live or she is not strong enough, the vet can cut her open and free the puppies that way, but then they would not have their mother.

Lexi wanders away from my hand. I hear his slippers. Her toenails click down the hall and pause where she finds my father. The scraping stops almost immediately after the clicking stops. "Weight shifts to the inside foot," my father says as if he were making it happen. His body never moves during a swing. "Head still. The arms and hands roll over. Right elbow folds under and points to the ground. Shift weight left. Unwind. Swing through. Head still. Then look."

Sometimes on Sunday afternoons over tea, my father and I argue quietly about dogs—their function and how they should be raised. When I was young and since then, we have always had dogs. I am full of theory; he is full of experience. My father would say that a dog is a voucher for one human life, nothing more. If you're not careful when training a dog, he would say, he will grow to believe what you believe, fear what you fear. Then he is of no use to you. When properly trained, a dog will ignore what he knows to be true in order to please you. He will go where you are afraid to go. This is what my father would say.

When they found a tunnel, my father sent the tunnel dog down first. They were never allowed to blow the tunnels up until they first searched for prisoners, maps, battle plans, or caches of weapons. Using dogs was apparently my father's idea for saving men. The dog was trained to detect the presence of living humans and return through another entrance to the Vietcong's underground complex. It had to be a small dog in order to maneuver well in the narrow tunnels that were often too small for many men to pass through. If the dog returned and barked twice, my father or someone else would go down through the tunnel with a flashlight and a .45. If the dog didn't return, sometimes they'd blow the tunnel up against orders, and sometimes my father would have to go down and see anyway. In 1968 he lost thirty-five dogs, but he saved thirty-five men.

My father's slippers scrape down the hall to the living room, where he pauses in the gray light. Lexi stops behind him, feebly raising her head to the back of his legs. He turns to me and sits down in the rocking chair. He purses his lips and hangs his hand off the end of the armrest. Lexi nestles her nose into his fingers, which run over her snout as she walks forward. She pauses where his hand sits on the back of her neck.

"I don't think we should wait any longer," he says.

"What do you mean?" I pretend not to know what he's talking about.

He reaches into his robe and pulls out the old, tarnished military-issue .45. He points it, butt first, at my hand. "Do you want to do it, or do you want me to do it?"

"I see no reason," I reply.

"Do you see this dog?" He raises his voice, the gun still held out in front of him. "It is already dead. Do you understand?"

"There are the puppies," I say.

He pulls the gun back into his lap and tilts his head toward the front window. "Don't make her suffer—she will not live to have those dogs."

"She might," I say.

"You know that's not true," he says. "And even if she were to, they would die without the mother."

"I will raise them myself," I say.

"Don't be ridiculous," he yells and stands up. "You're not a dog. You have no idea what you're doing." He pauses then, turns away from me and back once more. "It is God's will that life be taken away," he says.

"I've been reading about raising these dogs," I say weakly, thinking of the vet's prediction that Lexi would not live another three weeks, while there are at least six weeks until the puppies could be born.

My father turns his back to me and slips the gun back in his pocket. Lexi watches his every move. "It's your dog," he says and starts back down the hall. I lean forward to put my hand behind

Lexi's ears, but she stands up and follows my father. She was his dog before she was mine.

In 1968 my father was the golf champion of Qua Trang Province, but now he works over in the basement of City Hall selling Mars bars to people overdue on their parking violations and whatnot. When I used to work down on Middle Street selling vacation packages to places I couldn't afford to visit, we would have lunch together twice a week at the Front Street Deli.

Things are different these days. I used to be a travel agent, then I worked in a lab, and now I am looking for work. When I was very young my father and I would go fishing north of the paper mills, but I can hardly remember those times; he is hardly the person I would want to remember. We used to attend church twice a week. Over the years, even while my mother was alive, I stopped attending church, while he believed all the more. Since my mother's death he no longer believes but still goes to church two, sometimes three times a week, while I will never set foot in church again.

We studied the Bible every night after he had returned from the war when I was seven. My mother, father, and I would sit around a table. After the war, my father always read with his eyes shut, his thick, dark fingers dancing over the oversized Braille Bible he'd been given at the army hospital after he was wounded. We read it together, cover to cover, several times, but by the time I could even partially understand what was being said, my father had decided to keep us focused on Job. He cited the price of rent and groceries, the number of murders in our neighborhood, and what he called world economic downturn as examples of the inevitable return of Christ. He cited Job's corruption as an example of why Christ would have to return. At night I lay awake in bed picturing Christ wearing a robe and sandals, the blood still pouring from his hands and feet, picking up my friends from the neighborhood and tearing off their limbs. When I finally did fall asleep I often had a dream about walking along a sidewalk in front of our house when suddenly the ground would give out beneath me and I would be plunged into a volcano of fire. I would wake screaming and would continue screaming until my mother came running down the hall and placed her cool hand across my forehead.

Every Sunday I kneeled and ate of the body of Christ, the man who would come for me, and then I drank of his blood for reasons I could not understand. With the wafer sitting under my tongue, I looked up at the cross and the sculpture of his naked, starved, and bleeding body. I could only assume that I had been somehow responsible for the suffering of this great man, and that someday he would make me pay. I did not understand then that it was God that made him pay.

One Sunday morning as I knelt with the wafer in my mouth waiting for the cracked and dried hands to pass with the silver chalice, I sealed my lips shut. When the chalice paused before me, I stared straight ahead at the pulpit and would not open my mouth. The chalice waited for a second, the wine poised on the edge, until the hands moved on. Without realizing it, I had decided that I would no longer kneel before a man to whom I had done nothing, who would punish me no matter what I did. The next week when my father woke me for church, I told him that I would not go.

"Are you sick?" he asked, staring directly at me even though he could not see. In Vietnam, he had once told me, they had learned on night patrol to see with their ears. I could hear my mother shuffling back and forth downstairs. "You don't sound sick."

"I'm not sick. I'm just not going anymore."

"You're going," he replied and left the room. He returned a few minutes later and grabbed my arm, pulling lightly. "Come on," he asked politely—something he had never, to my knowledge, done before. I dug my fingers into the side of the bed. He turned around and faced the door. Then he flipped suddenly around again, grabbed my leg, and hauled me off the bed. The back of my head crashed against the floor, but I would not stand.

"Stand up!" he screamed at me.

"I'm not going," I said.

"You're going!" he screamed, reaching down for my arm and yanking me to my feet.

"I'm not going—ever again!" I screamed at his face. Very suddenly and without warning, he squared off and slapped me in the face. He was accurate even without being able to see. I suppose the military had trained him for that. I fell to the floor and could not open my eyes nor think straight. By the time I was able to walk downstairs, he and my mother had gone off to church. We never talked about it again, I never attended church again. We stopped the nightly readings from the Bible. Whatever thoughts he had about the end of the world were kept inside his head, which was fine with me.

Over the years I reread Job on my own dozens of times and carefully considered the pronouncements my father had made. At one point, sometime in my teens, long after my mother's death, I sat down with him and tried to present my case.

"First of all," I remember saying to my father that morning, "what is Job's sin?"

"What are you talking about?" my father asked, his breakfast half finished. I did not know that he no longer believed the things he had told me when I was seven.

"This is what God Himself says about Job in the beginning:

'Hast thou considered my servant Job, that there is none like him in the earth, a perfect and upright man, one that feareth God, and escheweth evil?' That there is none like him."

My father held his fork next to his plate of half-finished eggs.

"There is no one more innocent than Job, so what was his sin? That he questioned a God who was tricked by Satan into punishing him—that was his only crime."

My father stood up, put his plate in the sink, and returned to his bedroom. I heard the door click shut and the radio chatter. I sat at the table and continued my argument, sure, at the time, that his exit signaled defiance. It seemed important for me to finish.

"God's defense is no better than the ramblings of Job's friends. They all offer the same excuse, even though God claims that His answer is different. And I tell you what," I said, "Job knows this. He doesn't say so in the end, but he does. It's obvious." I had been waiting for more than seven years to possess the language and understanding to defend that morning I had refused to drink the wine from the chalice. When I finally finished my speech, I took up my Bible and returned to the living room, knowing full well that my defense had not been enough.

My father takes five steps down the hall, turns, and takes four steps into his bedroom. On days when he works, he takes fifty-seven strides to the bus stop (ten to the sidewalk, forty-seven straight to the left down the walk). Off the bus there are ninety-three steps to City Hall. Seventy-nine strides to the front entrance and then twenty-two stairs. He reverses this procedure to return home. Then on Saturdays and on certain days off he pauses at three o'clock to count his knives and also his spoons. On average he washes his face from four to six times a day. Groceries and supplies are delivered.

Sometimes before bed, I walk by my father's house and stand across the street. At ten twenty-five I can see him walking along the perimeter of each room, touching the table and chair my grandfather made in his shop. He turns the lights off, and on moonlit nights I can see his outline making steady headway down the hall into the windowless, pitch-dark center of the house.

At night when I am at my own home I think mostly about dogs. From books I know that the ideal collie stands twenty-two to twenty-six inches tall at the shoulder, weighs seventy-five pounds, and has a majestic air that borders on aloofness. To achieve this every collie should be kept on a regular feeding schedule and kept just a little bit hungry at all times. But there is much more, like frequent nail clipping and occasional bathing. Training ultimately depends on how intelligent you are and how intelligent your dog is. Think as your dog thinks, and he will understand you. The most important words in your dog's vocabulary: heel, sit, come, stay. When giving these commands use the shortest phrase and use the same word with the same meaning at all times.

Short, frequent lessons work better. Train before breakfast, then your dog assumes that the meal is a reward. You may teach him the lying-down maneuver, you may teach him the envied trick of staying parked outside a store for hours, only budging for you, but remember that collies have a natural tendency to chase anything that moves. Once the dog is allowed to practice this habit, it may be very difficult to break your collie of it. Any dog may run away, but a good dog will return home. If nobody's there, he will wait.

My father follows the wall to the foyer table, over to the counter, and back into the kitchen. After a few moments he starts down the hall toward me. Lexi follows right behind. "I got stuck in the rough on the eighth. Had to draw it out," he says. "People think they know how to play golf, but they have no idea." Lexi presses her nose against my leg, nudging me until I take her head in my hand and start stroking behind her ears.

"The first thing," he says, "once you have your clubs, is to choose your grip. The Vardon grip," he says, his hands wrapped around air. "Or the interlocking grip." The fingers mingle together. "Or the baseball grip, not used much anymore. If you don't know what club to use or what grip to take, wait and it will come to you. The other thing people don't know," he says, "is that you should never move your head. Keep your head steady at all times. If your head isn't steady, the ball will not know where you want it to go."

I nod my head.

Lexi jolts, her ears stand up, and she walks cautiously to the front door. She looks out the window. A dog senses out there what we can only guess at. I think back over what I've been reading about dogs and I look at my dog and think: What a dog stands on is more like a foot than a paw. The metatarsal bones may fall short in length, but, as with humans, the tibia falls into the tarsal bones, and the phalanges reach forward into the next step, curling into the earth for support. She turns her head back to look at me. Sometimes when I am too afraid, I remind myself of all the dog lives in her, and how they depend on what I do.

To raise happy dogs, in my opinion, it is important to be happy, and I have considered many forms of happiness. On certain days off, I take out an hour to sit on the edge of my roof looking down the hill toward where Broadway turns into Fort William's Ave. From there, I can see almost everything that people do. I think I have come to understand that most people's lives are no larger than my own.

My father reaches over to his left and pulls one of his pipes down from its cradle. He pulls a brown leather pouch out of his pants pocket and digs out some of the earthen material. He packs it in with his thumb, lights a match, holds it atop the pipe with his thumb and forefinger, and takes quick puffs until the smoke bellows out of his mouth.

Before bed each night, he sits in his chair smoking his pipe and listening to 93.8 FM. He has one pipe for each day and a spare one in case of accidents. Only on days off does he smoke it during daylight hours. Today the pipe lights but then goes out. He takes it out of his mouth, holds it in front of his face, then places it back in the cradle.

After a long silence, my father picks up one of Lexi's paws and runs his hand along the bones, then along the front leg, then along the flank. I stare into his blank, circled eyes. A couple years after he returned from Vietnam my father shot our family dog. I was nine at the time, the dog thirteen. One morning I found my father in the living room, his body wrapped around the dog's body. My father's chest heaved and his arms and legs seemed to tremble as he clenched his blind eyes shut and bared his teeth in the kind of grief that looks like rage. At nine I could not understand as he led the dog I had known for my entire life outside into the backyard, held a gun to the side of her head, and blew her brains all over the back lawn. Over time I have come to understand a part of what he knows, but at that moment I flew out the door into the yard screaming and throwing my fists at him, who thought he had been alone. He held my arms to the sides of my body until I calmed, and then he tried to explain that the dog had become old and ready to die. I did not know then or now how he decided this. And looking at the circles under his eyes, I think there may be things I know about despair that even he does not understand. The nature of the blackness that creeps into the mind and body from some unknown source is that it stays precisely as long as you can take it and then leaves suddenly, but with a promise of return visits. Many people who can take the blackness itself are killed by the promise of its return. The smallest details, daylight and the pipe in its cradle, become intolerable in anticipation of that darkness returning. And when I say despair will stay just as long as you can take it, that threshold is only seen in retrospect. At the time, you ask yourself every minute how much longer you can go on, and some people are never able to find out.

From his letters to my mother I know that golf ended for my father on October 5, 1968, when he left the rear base of Da Nang and headed for a small firebase somewhere in Qua Trang Province, the northern tip of South Vietnam. No one played golf because everyone lived underground. He hid beneath sandbags in the one-square-mile base. He was ten days into an attack by the Vietcong, who had completely surrounded them. He would go for ten more days before seeing the sun, and each night as part of the reconranger team he would lead a patrol to locate the position of the enemy. Then on January 3, 1969, he lost one of his dogs down a tunnel. The dog went down, according to his letter to my mother, and they waited for ten minutes but nothing happened. He had the choice of sending someone down who had never been before or going down himself, so he went. He wore a T-shirt, pants, and boots, carried a .45, a knife, and a small flashlight. After dropping down, he crawled along a horizontal corridor, no more than three feet tall, measuring the distance traveled in his mind, until he reached an intersection. He paused before it, shining the flashlight all around, checking for prints, human or canine, in the dirt, and then he just listened for a while. He heard nothing, so he moved forward. When he had reached the very edge of the intersection, there was a scuffle to his right. He aimed the .45, but it was too late. The man had his hand on the pistol and was pulling it toward him. My father pushed back the other way, but the other man was stronger, and the gun was pressed sideways against my father's face when it went off. It blinded him, but it killed the other man. If the other man had not been killed, my father would have been.

My father leans down again, running his hand along Lexi's flank. "What is it you would do with all these small dogs?"

"Give them away."

He nods. "I'm very tired," he says.

I nod. He rises, walks three steps to the edge of the room, fifteen down the hall, three into his bedroom, and then closes the door. In a few moments he will be asleep. It's dark now, Lexi's eyes closed at my feet, and the lights up and down the lane are starting to move from the first floors of people's houses to the upstairs bedrooms.

I was the kind of person who promised people anything and gave them what they got. It often occurs to me at night that I have not been a person in whom people have recognized a great deal of potential. I listen to classical music on the radio but don't remember the names of the composers. I wear nice shoes. Nine times out of ten, for me, happiness amounts to the interval between the absence of pain and the onset of boredom. In that sense I'm like everyone else, I suppose. I could say that today is the first day of the rest of my life and start anew, but I have said that countless times before.

These last three years since I have been clean, when I have gone out for coffee and a movie, sometimes I giggle, sometimes I'm morose. I laugh hysterically during the scenes when people's limbs are ripped off. When I dance to the radio in my bedroom my feet jut out and back, and my hands move over my thighs like crabs. I occasionally wear a cowboy hat in private and once every month or so smoke cigars. I worry that there might be someone like me out there thinking the things that I think.

I live alone in a one-story house at the end of a long street, and it has been the nature of my moodiness after work to walk through the empty bedrooms at night. It occurred to me in one of those rooms that I am not someone whose belief amounts to much. I have been able to see few miracles. I'm unemployed now, but in my last job I worked in a lab, and by and large miracles were not a part of my experience. With the little formal education that I have, I worked my way from the packing department, sending off test tubes, to a kind of low-grade, lab-coat-wearing technician with no real responsibility. After work I would rush home because Lexi would have been inside all day. I would feed the dog. After walking her at night I'd thank God and climb into bed.

I have been anxious and troubled, yet curious. As a former lab technician, I recognize in the world around me a certain degree of order that suggests an even greater degree of order that has not been explained and will never entirely be explained. Don't misunderstand me. I have not been a party to such burning-bush experiences as eventually draw people out there to California. The job of the mystic and the job of the scientist are nearly the same. By scientist I don't mean people like myself, who are the clergy of numbers, but the scientist to whom nothing seems adequately explained, who tears down and rebuilds our concept of the universe.

Any fool can see that God is not just, or if He is, then we are talking about a kind of justice which would make it impossible for many of us to live in the world. If God is love, as I would like to believe, then God is blind, unthinking, and vengeful—untrustworthy and jealous. Maybe it is our responsibility to forgive God. We are the ones, it seems to me, who must act with grace, turn away from our enemies, bury lust in the pit of the stomach, carry hope to each other like salesmen, door to door, and in the end be grateful.

What if Christ lied to us up until the last moments of his life? "What manner of man is this, that even the wind and the sea obey him?" asked his disciples. Only someone who knew the ugly truth about God could have created a lie that humanity would believe. Knowing that he would be punished, Christ still called out, "My God, my God, why hast thou forsaken me?" The answer is unacceptable, which is why even Christ had to lie to himself in order to live his life. The cry, let out moments before his father had mercy and released him from the world, was itself a relinquishing of the lie. I do not deny that Christ's power comes from God's Love; the secret is that God became jealous of His son. For Christ practiced Love with the kind of grace, justice, and humility that God has been able to exhibit only sporadically and without resolve. As Christ found, the price of defying the father is always self-destruction.

At night when Lexi and I would walk before she became too weak, I would try to follow the path that her nose takes along the streets that wind downtown from my neighborhood. She seems to be led by the odors that other dogs have left behind and by the odors of other animals, cats and mice. Even though she is sick now, when she can hear their little feet in the bushes, every muscle yanks against the leash. City dogs live, by necessity, like prisoners. Because I feed her every day, the purpose of our walking ritual is the ritual itself, and it does not seem to bother her that the tugs against the leash are merely token protests. You cannot curb a millennium of instinctual behavior by explaining that plenty of dog food will be provided, that she does not need to catch her own food.

Every morning I ask for God's help and I wait but there is no answer. I listen throughout the day, but no answer comes. It has occurred to me that of the people who ask for God's help, most receive no answer that they can understand. I may not know how to listen. So I try harder, asking down on my knees that my life be blessed with the kind of love that does not destroy, and yet I have no faith in my ability to tell the difference between one kind of love and another. The most important thing I do each day is feed the dog and the dog lives lying in Lexi's abdomen. When I rise in the morning and late at night, when I am trapped in my own thoughts, this is the only truth I know. I know that the kind of love that carries me home to my dog is the kind of love I hope for God. Love without desire.

When I was lying in detox in a New York hospital, my father sat by my side for the thirty hours it took me to regain consciousness; and when I woke he leaned over my ear and asked: "Are you awake?" I nodded my head. "Lay down your weapons," he told me, "and ask for God's help." I did. I asked for God's help but I could not lay my weapons down because I did not know what that meant. From the moment, however, after I declared on my knees that I did not know the first thing about how to live, my life seemed to take on a certain clarity. For the six months in the hospital and for several years afterwards the path out of my previous life seemed clear. And for that I thanked God every night. I have no idea why my father was able to make that one trip on the bus to see me in New York, why he managed to do one day what he had not been able to do for the previous eight years and has not done in the years since. But I do understand that he could ask me to place my life in the hands of a God that he himself no longer trusted, because in the end it only mattered if I believed what he was saying, which I did.

More recently, before breakfast after I wake, during the day, in my sleep and in the half-waking moments throughout the night, I obsess about the needles, the smell of the stuff and the places where I did it and the people I called my friends; but I can imagine, in my dreams, the feeling I always chased but never found. Almost all my ideas are bad ones.

When Lexi and I walk these days when she is feeling stronger, I find myself taking her along the Eastern Prom, where I used to live before moving to New York, where I know some of my old friends are living the life I have been able to renounce. She walks more slowly every day. Last night we paused at the east end park. Though a dog, in my opinion, has no sense of beauty, except insofar as their own actions are beautiful to us, Lexi sat staring out at the sunset which spread like a fire across the watery horizon. My eyes were trained down on the park where a group of people stood huddled around each other in the shadows of a hundred-year-old oak tree. When I rose this morning, rolled over on my knees, and spoke to God, my mind was still trained on those people down in the park. I can define myself by little else than the object of their desire. Though I try to spend my days thinking of nothing but walking Lexi, I become exhausted.

In August of my tenth year my mother took her own life with one of my father's guns. It seems that all the events of my life, both before and after, have been moving away from and back toward that August morning. Many years after her death, waking up in the hospital in New York, I realized I had traveled full circle and come to know the kind of isolation and confusion that my mother had known and could no longer bear. By way of explaining the outrage I felt in that hospital I could tell you about the months leading up to her death, the sitting with her at the kitchen table listening to her delusional talk about the neighbors spying on her, people plotting to kill her. I watched her pull down the blinds and hide, sobbing, under the kitchen table. I have gone over my nine-year-old's arguments a countless number of times, but I have never decided what I could have said to contend with her false beliefs. I have since come to understand that delusions contain within them the kind of love that allows us to live, even if those delusions eventually kill us. By this I think I mean that it is necessary not only to lie but to believe the lie.

I'll tell you the kind of love story that I believe. I was five years old and I hated nursery school. My mother hated taking me there. On the playground and in the classroom I spoke to no one. I know these things from what has since been told to me about myself. What I do actually remember is walking along the edge of the playground, kicking stones near the mesh fence. I leaned down to pick up a stone—I can see it now, a mixture of vanilla white and crystal. At that moment the recess bell rang, and I started to run for the building with the stone in my pocket. I felt suddenly full of power. At the end of the day, lying in bed, I handed the stone to my mother. She turned it around, held it up to the bed light. She placed it in her pocket, shut the light off and vanished into the dark hallway.

Every day now I am running across the field, identical to all the other kids except for the secret I carry in my pocket, and I wait through the rest of school and arrive home but no one is there. If there were someone there, she would not understand. She would say, "What is this?" And I would have to say, "You're right. I am too late." I do not know whether I am eight or twenty-eight.

While I descended the stairs and walked to the day camp bus on that August morning, my mother turned into the empty house and my father paused at the curb, waiting for a ride to work from one of his friends. There were many days when I turned back from the bus and spent the day with her because I was afraid of what might happen. On that day I ignored my fear, not because I thought nothing would happen, but because I lost hope in my own ability to love my mother enough. So I climbed the stairs of the bus, thinking over all the things I had said to her, hoping she would remember them. It was a musty, humid morning. When the bus arrived at the reservoir we filed off and wandered slowly down into the lukewarm water. When the water reached my knees, I stopped and felt as though I could not breathe.

My father found her later that day, but no one from the neighborhood knew what had happened nor cared to ask when the ambulance arrived to take the body away. Because the news did not reach beyond our house it never left our house. And when I came home to discover what had happened, I rushed at my father as I had on the day he had killed our dog. I did not understand and still do not why he had not been able to prevent her death and why, in my own mind, it had become my responsibility and my fault. I ran into his stomach and started punching him as hard as I could. The distance between my father and me and the distance between us and the rest of the world grew larger with every year until I could not be sure if I had not actually been responsible for her death. I could no longer separate what actually had happened from my worst fear of what had happened.

When she grabbed my hand before I boarded the bus the morning that she died and squeezed the blood out of my palm, my mother was reaching across a distance that no amount of love could bridge. So when I walked sternly across the playground with that stone, the gift of love, burning in my pocket, that in the end could not be received, it was swallowed by the distance that grew between my mother and the rest of the world.

When I think of my father and what he could have done to save my mother, as I always do sitting alone in his living room, I think of this story about a time before Vietnam when the future events of our lives lay just beneath our skin. I must have been five and my little cousin was eight when my father took us canoeing down the Allagash River. I fished all day and caught nothing. Toward the end of the first day, we paddled hard across Long Lake in order to reach the camp on the opposite shore before the orange horizon sank. On the second day it rained but we pushed downriver anyway. In the late afternoon I dropped the fishing rod overboard. My father stretched his long body out over the water but could not grab the rod before it sank. He succeeded instead in tipping the canoe over. My heavy rubber boots dragged me feet first right to the bottom. The surface of the water lay two feet above my head, but I could not move. I saw my cousin's flailing arms and my father's thick legs, his chest, shoulders, and head rising above the water into the air where I wanted to be. His hands closed around my cousin, lifting her out of the water, and then his legs moved away. In a few moments I stood alone underwater, and in my memory it seems that I accepted my situation absolutely. I accepted that my father would not return, as of course he would, and in those few moments I felt relieved to experience the kind of aloneness that my mother must have felt, that I would come to expect and that I would spend many years inflicting on myself.

Moments after a calm befell me I saw my father's distorted outline above the rippling window of the water's surface, and then I saw the legs moving underwater toward me. Finally I saw the hand crash down from the sky and grab me by the collar.

For many years I could not reconcile the force that drove his legs away from me, his love for his brother's daughter, and the force that drove his legs back to me, his love for me. It seemed impossible that two such forces, one evil, one good, could coexist. And if they did, how was I to anticipate which force would dominate my life? Only recently have I been able to see that the same love which drove my father away from me drove him back moments later. I knew, standing on the bottom of the river at five years old, when I saw my father's distorted image descending from above, that I was not forsaken, but I have never been able to understand, on some level, why his power to steal life back was extended to me but not my mother. I have always been in awe of the illusion of this power to give and take life at whim, and that I am alive because this love favored me.

I wish I could say with any degree of certainty that desire, the kind of love that crushes at the same time it empties, the kind of love that can never be fulfilled, is not the love of God. When I think back on those five or six years of my life that were consumed by a single obsession for a substance that nearly killed me, there is nothing that I like but everything that I want. When I feel this desire moving ferociously through me, as I do now and have for some time, I am most convinced that God loves me and is, at the same time, seemingly indifferent to my own destruction.

One night in New York I came to know about myself, God, and the world just what I desperately wanted to avoid. I was in a bar with people I knew down the street from my apartment on 43rd Street. A woman one of our friends knew sat down at a table with us. She pressed her lips together and nodded at me, and I remember nodding back to her. I raised a glass to my mouth, watching her lower lip, and then closed my eyes. There my memory stops until the next morning when I raised myself out of someone else's bed and looked down at the dirty street. Even when I turned around to find the woman I had met the previous night, her face covered with bruises, lying unconscious on the floor, I still could not remember what had happened. My one broken knuckle explained enough. I found my sneakers under the bed and pulled them on my feet. At the sink I cleaned my hands with dish soap. Finally, I checked the woman's pulse with my pinkie, found a beat, and crept out of the apartment. Later I called an ambulance from halfway across town. I sat on the street corner outside my friend's apartment. I sat there until well past dark. I knew then, as I know now, that I am capable of anything and that everything proceeds from a kind of love that knows no boundaries nor limits, that dwells in darkness as well as in light. There is no way of knowing, when I step into the world today, whether I will go back to that life. There is no way of knowing what kind of love the world will suffer at my hand, and sometimes there is not enough time in one life to understand the consequences of what I have done.

And what could I do when my friend with his glazed-over eyes came tumbling down the front steps and asked me to come inside where some people were sitting around a room in the dim light, their eyes half closed, smoke in the air? The knowledge of what I had just done should have guided me. Though I did not ask for help, I did pause and wait for the right answer as if time would sort out the truth and save me from myself. What excuse can I give now except that I bowed my head and walked up into the apartment because it was the only thing I knew how to do.

Lexi, who has been lying paw over paw in front of the fire, suddenly raises her head, straightens her ears, and barks at the door. I stand up and pause behind her. There is a level of despair that cannot be communicated by words. I recognize in Lexi's bark the tenor of this despair. She turns and walks cautiously down the hall toward my father's room. I hear the swishing of his slippers slowly making their way toward me. Craning my head away from the front window, I wait for his face to emerge from around the corner. He stops so that half his face and body are concealed by the wall, tilts his head in my direction, and not finding me there, tilts it toward the other side of the room. Finally he turns and drags his slippers back down the hall. Lexi's toenails click after his heels to where, in the kitchen, I find him pulling dog biscuits out of the cupboard. He leans over, running his hand along the side of her face. She presses against him and opens her mouth to receive the present.

My father hears me pause by the sink and pour myself a glass of water. He straightens his back and leans against the cupboard, pulling the bathrobe across his old chest. "I couldn't sleep," he says. I nod. "Would you like some tea, or do you have to go?" he asks. And even though I am tired and have to rise early to look for work, I push away from the sink and, moving toward the stove, say, "Why don't you sit down while I make the tea?" But he has already lifted the pot and laid it down on the stove.

On the kitchen counter sits his old military .45. I cradle the gun in my hand as Lexi nudges her nose against my leg and lies down, resting the uneaten biscuit by her face. She lets out a sigh that becomes a whine, her body shuddering with each breath. I run my hand along the top of her head. She has laid herself at my feet.

Lifting the teapot from the stove, my father hears me pulling the slide back on the .45 as I have seen him do dozens of times over the years, slipping the cartridge into the chamber. He turns the gas off and replaces the pot on the burner, his hands bracing against the stove front as I open the back door and lead Lexi out into the yard. When I stop walking, she collapses at my feet, closing her eyes.

In that tunnel with this gun, I believe I would have died. I have spent too many days in struggle against myself to think that I could win against another human being in a fight for my life. A man who has had a gun to his own head may not be able to turn it against someone else, possibly because he knows there is no such thing as killing the enemy. I am afraid that I am still a child and may never become the kind of man who is strong enough to relieve suffering by removing life.

I lean down, rub her ears, and ask myself what a dog could know about the predictions and explanations given by a vet. Though I have been lucky enough to live a life I can partially explain to myself, there seems little hope in the end of explaining the absence of life, even if it does mean a respite from pain. I rest my head against the back of Lexi's head, hoping that she will speak through her faltering breath, and guide me, but she cannot. Nor does my father, standing above the sink with his eyes closed, lift his head or utter a sound. I wait a moment longer, as I once waited when I was five on the bottom of the river for my father's hand to crash down through the water, and I wish I could ask him, what kind of love grows out of a lie? Does it falter, will it rot any sooner? Lying to him is the only way I know how to live. Maybe if I were the kind of person who could find truth buried in his own chest, I would not need to lie in order to hide the kind of love he will never understand. Placing one hand on the back of Lexi's head, I raise the gun in the air and pull the trigger against the sky.

CPSIA information can be obtained
at www.ICGtesting.com
Printed in the USA
LVHW050224080222
710484LV00006B/362